Eye Kill

by

Ido Graf

Also, by Ido Graf

In the Adam Wolf series:

'Eye Kill'
'See Glass' - Repeated **Amazon Best Seller** in Multiple
Categories, Internationally.

Short Stories:

'Ukraine Rising'
'Bar None'
'My Mercedes' – Coming soon.
'Latin Jack' – Coming soon.

I dedicate this novel with the deepest affection to:

Paul and Gwyneth

To friendship!

'Bond ordered a double gin and tonic and one whole green lime. When the drink came, he cut the lime in half, dropped the two squeezed halves into the long glass, almost filled the glass with ice cubes and then poured in the tonic.' Ian Fleming, Dr. No.

Fleming wrote the novel in early 1957 at his Goldeneye estate in Jamaica. It was filmed in London and on location in Jamaica in 1962.

'Fiat Justitia.'
Let Justice Be Done
Motto of the British Royal Air Force Police

Originally taken from:

'Fiat Justitia ruat caelum.'
Let Justice be done though the heavens fall.
Possible source:
Lucius Calpurnius Piso Caesoninus, (101 BC – c. 43 BC)

Media Requests & Film Rights

All press enquiries or film rights requests relating to Ido Graf's books should be directed to his publicist.

Any negotiations regarding the novels should be directed to his lawyers of choice in Washington D.C.

Please make any enquiries through the contact page.

https://www.idograf.com

ISBN: 978-1-9162140-6-4

Contents

Prologue
Bagram Air Base, Parwan Province,
Afghanistan

'The Americans kill our children!'

The phrase was one that he had repeatedly heard shouted at him and his fellow Marines. It was touted about by the Taliban to instil fear and hatred into the populace.

For some reason he couldn't keep it from his mind as he lay motionless on the hillside. He was staring through the scope of his sniper rifle at the boys and girls happily playing in the sun-baked village at the base of the valley far below. He hoped that their lives would be as content in the future, but he had his doubts. That magnificent, remote, mountainous country had been fought over for centuries and the losers were always the children, one way or another.

His spotter and he had been staked-out for days in

the same location. Their nest had been a shallow depression on the downward slope of a nondescript rock-strewn mountain. As he lay there, he often dreamt longingly of the refreshing rains of home, to rinse away the dry dust which caked him.

Each afternoon he had watched hypnotically as two Egyptian vultures circled high above the valley floor kept aloft by the rising thermals. The bird's plumage should have been predominantly white with black flight feathers, though the white had turned a rusty cream - coloured by dust from the parched landscape. They were silent, calming, and graceful and above all, patient. He was patient too.

The wait had been worth it. Nearing the end of their mission a battered, blue car had raced into the village. As they watched, one of the men who had emerged from the vehicle was identified as a high value target. It was not who they had been expecting to see, but he was on their kill list. The terrorist had been born in the village, and he was greeted like a long-lost friend by the adults and by their children. Though it was not evident, their effusive welcome was in large part out of fear of the man.

Whilst the spotter watched the target and gave information to the marksman a commotion above them, near the brow of the hill, drew their attention. A group of Taliban had been searching the area to protect their visitor. They were among many who had been sent up into the hills earlier that day to search for infiltrators. The Marines had held their fire in the hope that the men would move on. However, when one of the Taliban came close to a Lance Corporal's hiding place and the soldier was sure to be discovered, he let go a burst of silenced machine gun fire into the man's chest. As the Afghan fell, dying, his trigger finger clenched and let off a burst of bullets from his AK-47 one of which went through the thigh of the soldier. The other Marines instantly engaged in unison ripping through the Taliban force which had been caught unawares. Though the Afghans tried to retaliate, the Marines were in a strong defensive position, and they had a perfect field of fire. When the firefight was done, none of the Taliban remained alive. A private signalled to the spotter to indicate that things were secure and that they were calling in a helicopter. The sniper turned to his buddy and said, 'Let's finish what we were sent here to do!'

As he nestled back into his scope he breathed in deeply and then slowly exhaled. As he did so he noticed a faint scent emanating from the tiny mountain flowers which dotted the hillside. Oddly, the musky smells had a deeply cleansing and calming effect.

The target and his accomplice, in the valley below, grabbed a nearby villager for cover at the first sound of gunfire. They ran back to the car forcing the individual into the rear seat despite the wild protestations of a nearby group of women. The vehicle raced back out of the village along the dirt track spraying rocks and dust everywhere. It made the desperate onlookers duck for cover, protecting their children as they did so. The car slewed and twisted as the driver tried to stay on the road and to make them a more difficult target.

The spotter called out elevation, wind, and range estimation and then there was silence as the sniper slowly exhaled and brought his heartbeat down as low as possible. His eye burrowed through the scope deep down towards the valley floor as the barrel gently tracked in unison with the car's movements. First, he shot the driver through the windscreen, which brought the car to a skidding stop. The passenger in the front seat, who was the main target, leapt out of the door and ran for cover, but the terrorist was shot through the chest before he had taken four steps. The shooter fired another volley into the man's unmoving skull to make sure that he was dead and then turned his attention to the person in the rear of the car. The individual had jumped from the vehicle and had made his escape. As the sniper followed the target, he saw that he was a boy of maybe twelve or thirteen – the unwilling hostage. Just as his training had taught him his breathing slowed down and he reduced his heartbeat, as the barrel followed the child, as if he were an automaton. However, his finger had purposefully slipped away from the trigger. Then the barrel stopped moving as the target continued to run. Frantic women and men, on seeing the child's plight, had raced towards the boy screaming hysterically as they went. Many of them looked imploringly up the slope towards the Marines. The sniper had seen many children murdered during his tour in Afghanistan. But they had been intentionally killed by the terrorists and not the Americans. Each child's killing gave him renewed determination to avenge those deaths.

Adam stood up giving away his position and raising an arm, he gave a long slow wave to the people below. By that time, the villagers had reached the child and the women had smothered him with their bodies. Sweat poured down the boy's face and back and he was trembling uncontrollably as his eyes stared up into the vast, rock slope. On seeing the Marine's gesture, Omar, the young boy, pushed himself free of the women and looking up at the soldier he returned a slow acknowledging wave in thanks for his life. Then the sniper team gathered their equipment and climbed rapidly up the slope. Within five minutes they saw the Black Hawk coming across the mountains heading directly towards them. It was homing in on the billowing clouds from the M18 smoke grenade which the Marines had thrown into a clearing which would act as the landing zone.

The Sikorsky UH-60 helicopter descended gently to the hilltop sending dust and sand skywards in large clouds across the landscape. Just before it touched down Marines, pulling their goggles over their eyes, emerged from their hiding places between the boulders. Most raced towards the open doors. Some held back to form a perimeter while the Lance Corporal with a badly wounded leg was helped on board by two privates. While they had waited one of them had applied a tourniquet to stem the blood flow and had roughly dressed the injury with a field dressing. Once the injured man was safely in place and the sniper and his spotter had jumped aboard the perimeter detail fell back to the helicopter. They then jumped on board and moments later the helicopter climbed skywards. The soldiers could hear small-arms fire from the valley below, but it was too distant to cause them any danger. Eventually the pockets of Taliban gave up their fruitless efforts. The flight took thirty-five minutes and though the air coming through the open doors did cool the men to an extent, they were still stiflingly hot. The days that the sniper team had lain hidden among the loose scree and rocks littering the mountainside had proved to be worthwhile. The Marines who had accompanied them and who had provided cover to the rear were very satisfied with the outcome once they were told who had been eliminated. They knew of the target who had been hit and all were certain that the target had much innocent blood on his hands.

The sniper was pulled from his thoughts as he subconsciously noticed a change in the sound of the helicopter as it began to reduce speed and descend towards the airbase. The Black Hawk was brought in for a very gentle landing and the Marines rapidly disembarked. The injured Lance Corporal was once again helped by the two privates who half carried him into a waiting ambulance. A Humvee pulled up beside the helicopter and the driver told Adam that the Major wanted to see him the moment he returned. Adam placed his sniper rifle and pack in the back of the vehicle and climbed in. He glanced over at his spotter and gave him a nod. Adam did not ask why the Major wanted to speak to him and they drove off in silence. On arriving at Major Martinez's tent, he jumped out and grabbed his weapon and kit before entering.

He was met by a Corporal who ushered him straight through, saying, 'The Major is expecting you, Sergeant.'

Adam noted that the Corporal had given him a curious look as he spoke. The sniper then walked in and saluted and as the Major saluted back he said, 'Please sit down Adam.'

Adam knew the officer relatively well, but even so he was very surprised by his informal tone and use of his forename.

The Major paused and drew in a deep slow breath before saying, 'I'm very sorry, but I have bad news for you.'

Adam said nothing and just looked straight back at

the officer as he continued, 'I've been informed that your brother, his wife and your niece and nephew have all been killed in a house fire.'

Martinez stared compassionately at Adam, and he was astonished to see no discernible emotion in the sniper's face. He presumed that the shock was so very great that he couldn't quite take it in, or possibly the Marine was not close with his family.

The Major continued, 'Sergeant, we have you scheduled on a flight this afternoon back to the States. If I can be of any help to you in the meantime, then please let me know? ...I'm really sorry!'

Adam looked thoughtful, and then said, 'Sir, can you tell me exactly what happened?'

The officer went to answer, and Adam thought momentarily that he looked unnerved.

The Major wasn't telling him everything, and Adam felt that he knew why.

Major Martinez hesitated before saying, 'I... I don't feel it's my place to speak to you about such matters. I'm not sure that I have all the facts. I have been informed that the local Sheriff will fill you in when you get to the town where your brothers family lived.'

Martinez thought that when he had mentioned the Sheriff, there had been some sort of recognition in Adam's face. There had indeed been recognition in Adam's demeanour. He certainly did know of him.

Adam thanked the Major and then saluted. As he left the tent and made his way back to his own quarters he was met by Amit. The bearded, middle-aged Afghan was the unit's translator. His face looked pained, and he spoke gently to Adam, 'I have heard about your family.' As Amit lay his hand on Adam's arm he continued sincerely, 'I will pray for them.'

Adam was deeply touched by the Afghan's words and by his kindness, but he replied cryptically, 'Thank you, but they are beyond prayers now, though others may need them!'

Amit watched as the sniper gave him a half smile before turning and walking away.

Just as he did so a dark cloud passed across the sun.

Chapter One
Three days earlier, Clintburg, Kentucky State, USA

The day had been hot, and it remained warm as evening fell. A gentle breeze intermittently gave welcome respite to the family who lay sleeping in the small wooden house. The building itself lay nestled among a grove of mature Pitch pines at the end of a short dirt track which came off the tarmacked road in a wide arch. The scent from the trees was overpowering.

It was early evening and the ever-present background noise of crickets and katydids masked most other sounds. The haunting call of a distant Northern barred owl abruptly and momentarily disrupted the insects chatter and served as a portent of doom, while the family slept on.

In the darkness, four men, dressed in camouflage pattern hunting outfits, slowly crept through the light undergrowth. Oddly, they did not carry hunting rifles – just pistols. The men had parked their grey Ford Raptor pickup truck half a mile away and a hundred yards down a little used logging road. The driver, Buck, took the time to turn the vehicle before they departed to make for a faster exit.

The group slowed as they came close to the edge of the track which led on to the house. Their heavy boots made some noise, though it was masked by the night sounds. The front man, Floyd, stopped just before the clearing in front of the house and the others followed his lead. Standing amid the pines he spoke softly to the other men, and they split into groups of two. Jeb stayed with Floyd, while Buck and Wade slowly made their way to the back of the property.

Once they were all in place the pairs moved silently towards the front and back doors respectively. The house was in darkness, but they were taking no chances. It was unusual in that rural area for people to lock their doors, but both the front and back entrances were not only locked – they had newly installed high grade security bolts fitted. A cursory glance at the windows was enough to inform even Floyd, that these were equally well pro-tected.

He sent Jeb to the back of the house to pass on a mes-sage to his compatriots. On Jeb's return Floyd stepped back from the door and raised his pistol aiming at the lock. The time for stealth had passed. He nodded to Jeb and then fired two shots into the lock, hearing the expected further shots at the back of the house. Jeb then burst through the splintered door, as he had been instructed, and raced up the stairs to the upper floor. Before he had reached the top a shot rang out and he stopped still before making a slow half turn and falling back down the stairs. Floyd cowered in the hall looking at the lifeless Jeb. The dead man lay, head down, halfway up the stairs, eyes unblinking with an angry red dot near the centre of his forehead. All Floyd could think was that it may well have been him lying there dead. Anyone who knew Floyd, however, would realise that there was never any chance of that as he always got others to do the dirty work. Floyd ran his hand hard across his mouth, as if to stifle a scream. His other hand began to tremble.

Floyd tried to send Buck and Wade up the stairs, but clearly reluctant, they chose to fire into the ceiling instead, aiming at the point where they thought the shooter would be lurking. After a series of shots, they heard a scream of pain and only at that point did they rush forward. On reaching the upper floor they were disorientated in the darkness, having foolishly forgotten to bring torches. Suddenly a flashlight shone into their eyes and three shots burst forth. Wade took two in the chest as he collapsed against the wall screaming in agony while Buck dived for the floor taking a hit in the shoulder. He cried out in pain but not before, in panic, he had let off a shot in the direction of the flashlight. The intruders were unused to firing at a creature of any sort which fired back. Seeing the flashlight fall, Buck ran forward in terror kicking his feet out until they hit flesh. Suddenly the landing light was switched on by Floyd who cautiously peered out from the top of the stairs. Floyd and Buck saw their quarry lying unconscious on the floor, a bullet wound in his leg and a bullet graze across his cheek.

Buck went to kick the prostrate man once more, only to be stopped by Floyd. The wounded Buck looked back along the landing and screamed out, 'Jeb's dead and look at Wade!'

Floyd was unconcerned with the other men and with a statement of the blindingly obvious.

'We will look after them later, Buck!' he said ominously in reply.

He stepped over the prostrate Wade and walked down the hall listening to the terrified screaming of a woman and children as he went.

'Grab him!' he said to Buck who with difficulty dragged the man into the room where the noise was coming from.

As they entered, they saw an attractive woman in her mid-twenties lying on the bed holding on to her two children – a girl and a boy both of about seven years old. The children hid their eyes while the woman looked on in horror at her unconscious husband as he was manhandled into a wicker chair in the corner of the room.

'You'd all better shut up, if you know what's good for you!' Floyd snarled, emboldened by the lack of any threat to himself.

'Buck, tie him up and gag him!' Floyd barked.

With great difficulty and some considerable pain Buck pulled rope from his pocket and tied the victim securely to the chair. Then, unasked, he took more rope and pulled the woman's left arm from the boy and roughly tied her wrist to the bedstead. Then he grabbed the boy and roughly threw him screaming off the bed followed by the young girl. The woman was in hysterics as Buck, never one to refrain from brutality towards women, smashed his fist into her face, before binding her other wrist securely and in the same fashion as before.

Floyd had left the room while this occurred and returned as Buck was making the last knot secure. Floyd held a bowl of water before him which he carelessly threw over the unconscious husband. This had the desired effect of bringing him around slowly. The man looked up, still groggy and just in time to see the smiling Floyd shoot both of his children dead.

The bound man, Danny, violently tried to break his bonds but with no success. Hysteria was written across his eyes.

His wife unable to comprehend the horror of it all, fell into a weeping stupor.

Floyd turned back to the husband and then said, 'You really should have kept out of our business!'

Turning towards the woman as he undid his belt, he said for all to hear, 'Now the real entertainment can begin.'

An hour later when they had finished, the woman lay bruised and brutalised on the bed. She was quite lifeless, her heart giving way part-way through the ordeal, as she had given up all will to live.

Danny remained bound to the chair with blood oozing from his wounds and from the cuts caused by the ropes where he had desperately tried to wrestle free.

He was no longer a man; he had morphed into a wild animal. His eyes glared at Floyd with the passion and intensity of a creature who no longer wished for life – one who was intent on wreaking a terrible vengeance before his last gasp left him.

Floyd who looked satisfied and smug sent Buck to get the pickup. On his return the men carried the lifeless Jeb and the critically injured Wade into the rear of the truck.

Buck said as they returned to the house, 'We need to get Wade to a hospital or he ain't gonna make it!'

Floyd passed him a quizzical glance but said nothing.

Buck was carrying a large can of gas that he had hauled out of the back of the truck. He busied himself covering the ground-floor of the house in fuel and then replaced the empty can in the pickup.

Floyd took a last chance to return to the upper floor to gloat over the ruined, dying man, before bounding down the stairs. He took a lighter from his pocket and went into the front room setting light to a curtain. As he did so flames burst forth knocking him backwards, fearful, and making him drop the lighter. Buck had certainly done his job well dousing everything in sight. Floyd ran out of the house tripping down the wooden steps before half falling off the porch. He had been flustered by the sudden burst of heat from the flames and by the smell of his own singed eyelashes and eyebrows.

Heart racing, he jumped into the passenger seat of the truck as Buck pressed the gas pedal whilst stones, kicked up by the tyres, peppered the house, which was by then fully alight.

Danny would never personally get the revenge he so desperately wanted. As he died in agony, a grim smile crossed his face. He thought of his family and knew that he would be united with them very soon. He also smiled because he knew that his brother, Adam, would return!

Thirty-five minutes later the Ford Raptor pulled up close to a cliff above a disused and flooded quarry.

Buck and Floyd manhandled Jeb's body to the cliff edge. They then filled his pockets and the inside of his coat with rocks and bound him like a parcel before throwing him into the depths.

'I feel bad 'bout this.' Buck said, 'I know Jeb's family real good! I don't know what I will tell them!'

Floyd was two steps behind him, when he fired two shots into Buck's back. The unknowing man fell to the floor as the life gradually ebbed out of him. Floyd rolled him over and looked into Buck's eyes as the light faded from them, 'You ain't going to be telling anybody 'anything' Buck!'

Floyd then packaged Buck up, just as they had Jeb, and tossed him into the water.

It had been a struggle to get Buck to the cliff's edge as he was built like an ox.

Floyd returned to the truck and then tried to awaken Wade from his torpor.

'Come on Wade, we need to get moving quickly!' He said encouragingly, so that Wade could help with transporting his own body to its final resting place.

Wade, suffering from severe blood-loss was helped from the pickup by Floyd as they staggered through the trees towards the void. Giving himself some respite from the pain the wounded man dreamt of happier times spent with his girlfriend when she was off duty.

Coming close to the edge Floyd said, 'Take a break Wade!' before helping to lower him to the ground.

Wade felt very cold, and he was fading in and out of

consciousness as Floyd busied himself stuffing the wounded man's clothing with rocks.

Suddenly, Wade, in a moment of clarity, thrust his hands forward violently, and grabbing Floyd's throat began to throttle the life out of him. Though debilitated, Wade's grip was incredibly powerful and came from years of logging and farm work. Floyd was in a desperate panic as he felt that he was certainly going to die. Then as suddenly as it had come the pressure on his neck released as Wade slipped back into unconsciousness.

Floyd fell back gasping for air before grabbing a rock and smashing it into Wade's head. Jumping up he hysterically and violently began to repeatedly kick the prostate body, which helped to release the terror he felt. Floyd's body shook uncontrollably, and he felt stone cold with skin that was suddenly wet with sweat. When he had calmed down, he continued cautiously with his preparations for Wade's final journey. Completing the work he dragged Wade, who still clung to life, to the edge and then kicked him over. It was with a sense of great relief that he listened to the momentary silence before hearing the great splash far below. Then the silence returned!

He walked back to the truck and went to drive off before realising that Buck must have put the key in his pocket. Left with no other option he rolled the Ford into the watery grave and began the ten mile walk back to town.

His mouth was dry, and he yearned for a beer, but it was to be a long time until he reached a bar.

Chapter Two
Wheeler-Sack Army Airfield, Fort Drum, New York State, USA

Adam had woken from his sleep an hour before the wheels of the enormous Lockheed C-5M Super Galaxy gently touched down at Wheeler-Sack airfield on the American East Coast.

The transport plane had left Afghanistan in the early hours with returning troops and equipment that was being shipped back Stateside. The aircraft was far from full, and the crew had given Adam a quiet, secluded seat some distance from the other soldiers.

The flight had been uneventful apart from a short stop when they had landed, to refuel, at RAF Brize Norton, Oxfordshire in central England. The relief crew, who had been sleeping in the accommodation area in the upper deck, had then taken over.

Adam took the chance to stretch his legs on the tarmac. As he drank a coffee, he looked out towards a distant cropless field. The taste of the instant coffee was bitter. The haunting sound of an unseen pheasant cut through Adam's thoughts. The soft drizzle which fell on his face felt refreshing, but it was also cold.

Though Adam had slept intermittently, he felt no sense of being refreshed. His brother and his family had been the only close relatives he had remaining. He was left with a void following their loss and a sick feeling in the pit of his stomach. A feeling that would not leave him.

However, more than anything, he was overcome with an inner, violent rage. Against what and against who, he could not say – but it was a rage that he intended to satisfy.

The aircraft had taken much of the runway to land in the US, before it slowly began to taxi over to the hangars.

As the Super Galaxy came to a halt one of the loadmasters, a USAF Staff Sergeant, came up to Adam and said, 'There's a Humvee waiting at the bottom of the ramp for you Sergeant.'

Adam responded wearily, 'Thank you, Staff Sergeant.'

Adam grabbed his kit and made his way to the open nose of the Lockheed and walked down the slope feeling a sudden gust of wind gently brush his face as he left the fuselage behind him. Ordinarily, on returning from active duty abroad, he would have a great sense of homecoming on feeling his boots touch the American mainland once more. He felt no such sensation on that occasion as the sole of his boot touched the concrete. Striding towards the vehicle he threw his kit into the back and then climbed aboard, nodding to the driver as he did so. An R-11 Refueler tanker with a full load of fuel passed by just as he was shutting his door and Adam was suddenly aware of an overpowering smell of aviation gas. The smell always reminded him of his time at Jump School in Fort Moore in Georgia where he had done his parachute training.

As the vehicle pulled away Adam looked up at the great beast of a transport plane with its nose pointing to the Heavens. It looked every bit like one of the playful Harbor seals that his brother and he had happily watched, as children, as the creatures lay sunning themselves on the jetties in San Francisco Bay. How he wished that he could transport himself back to those happy times.

When they had come in to land the sky had been dry but overcast, but as Adam stared wistfully out through the bullet-resistant glass, lost in his thoughts, it began to rain softly.

The private drew Adam from his memories saying, 'Sergeant, you've been billeted for the night in barracks with the 10th Mountain Division.' Adam wasn't surprised as Fort Drum was the main base for that specialist light Infantry unit. He had come across them many times before in the course of his service. They were very tough, and he had always found them to be a great bunch of guys.

However, Adam made no answer, and they drove the rest of the short journey in silence.

They passed by various military vehicles and marching, chanting, platoons of soldiers before the Humvee pulled up at a low, non-descript barracks.

He grabbed his kit and thanked the driver and as he turned towards his billet, he noticed a pretty, young Asian private striding towards him.

Coming to a halt she said kindly, 'Sergeant, I am sorry for your loss!'

After a short pause she continued, 'May I help you with your luggage?'

'Thank you Private. No, I am fine.'

'Please follow me, Sergeant' she said.

As they walked into the quarters, she gave him details of the general amenities on the base such as the location of the Chow Hall. Adam was then shown to a private room where she left him.

He dropped his kit and sank down onto the bed, closing his eyes as he did so. He tried to push away the happy memories of his brother and his family. But like a lazily, discarded boomerang they just kept returning. A great sadness wafted over him as did, surprisingly, an unexpected sense of utter despair.

Adam woke early the next morning, showered, dressed, and headed over to the Chow Hall where he ate heartily, finishing breakfast off with a strong black coffee.

He had endured an unsettled night but was keen to get on.

As Adam drank his coffee, he noticed the female private who had shown him to his room the previous day. She had entered through the main door and had come to an abrupt stop, while she scanned the room. On seeing Adam, she smiled and walked briskly towards him before saying, 'Good Morning, Sergeant. One of my friends is heading into town and she would be happy to drop you at the Greyhound station if you wish to catch a bus? I've also been asked to give you this travel pass.'

Handing the pass to him, she gave Adam a glowing smile saying, 'I can wait for you outside if you wish?'

He did wonder why she would need to wait for him, but he smiled inwardly for the first time since he had left Afghanistan, as he admitted to himself that he probably did know why.

'That's fine Private. I'm just about finished anyway,' he replied as he swilled down the last of the coffee and rose to leave.

As he did so one of the soldiers in the catering unit walked up to him and told him that he had received a telephone call. Adam thought it strange, but he followed the man's lead and was shown through to a phone in an office at the back of the hall.

Answering, he heard the welcome voice of 'Chief'. He was a full-blooded Cherokee, and his name was John Riggs, but he was affectionately called Chief by everyone in the unit. They had all come to value him highly. He seemed to have an innate ability for sensing danger, and he was the finest, natural soldier that Adam had ever known. He had been sent back to the States to recuperate three weeks earlier, as he had been shot in the leg during a firefight, while out on patrol.

'Hey Chief! How are you? How is the wound?'

'Fine! I will be glad to go back though! I've been putting on weight. My Mom thinks they don't feed me enough in the army!'

Adam laughed and asked how he had found him. Riggs explained that he'd heard about what had happened from some of the men in the unit and then it had been a simple matter of tracking him down.

'Adam, you know that I will help you in any way I can.'

Adam said softly, 'I know that Chief. Thanks. But I think I will be able to deal with this myself. Anyway, you need to get yourself fit again.'

Chief said nothing for a moment and then discussed with Adam what his plans were, and they agreed to meet up for a drink before they headed back to Afghanistan.

Just before he rang off Chief said, 'Did you hear about Amit?'

Adam, perplexed replied, 'No, what about him?'

'He was out on patrol in a village with the unit. Amit was translating for us with the village elders. When the team left the village, they were ambushed. Brett was hit badly in the knee by insurgents. Amit ran out to help him. He dragged Brett behind a low wall to protect him from fire. Amit was hit by a ricocheting bullet which hit him square in the temple before he could take cover himself. He died where he fell.'

At that moment, the brutal images of what had happened were imagined in Adam's mind.

He felt numb. Adam had liked and admired Amit and had only recently spoken to him. 'How is Brett'

'He is doing well. He would have been dead if it hadn't been for Amit.'

Adam thought of poor Amit and his wife and young family. They were 'dirt poor' and that was why he had become a translator – to give his family a better life. 'We must try to help his family. They will be targeted by the Taliban in the future.'

'I know!' Chief retorted. 'Don't worry. The C.O. is on it.'

They said their goodbyes and Adam stared thoughtfully at the receiver as he replaced it in its cradle. He wasn't the only person with worries he thought, as he remembered the translator's young family. Leaving the room, he found the young woman waiting for him.

They walked back to his accommodation, and he noticed a large, white RAM pickup truck stationed outside by the sidewalk with a uniformed young female soldier in the driving seat.

'Sergeant, that's my friend Chantel. She is happy to wait until later in the day if you wish, but I thought...' she dropped into a softer and more sombre tone, '...that given the circumstances you may wish to get on your way?'

'Yes. 'Now' would suit me Private,' he said, 'I'll just get my kit.'

He walked back to his room and was aware that she had followed him at a short distance. He packed his kit and went to leave, but as he moved into the corridor, he noticed the soldier waiting for him, smiling softly.

She began nervously, 'I'm very sorry that we have met in these terrible circumstances,' she whispered whilst leaving a respectful and momentary silence, 'but if ever you would like to meet again, then that would be ...wonderful!'

Forgetfully and abruptly, she added, '...um, Sergeant.'

He noticed that her cheeks had flushed lightly and that she anxiously glanced towards the floor as she spoke.

Adam looked at her flawless skin and her statuesque, chiselled features coupled with a truly magnetic personality.

Adam leant forward and kissed her softly on the cheek saying, 'Thank you for your kindness and yes, that would be ...wonderful!' Joking he added, '...um, Private!'

She gave him a broad smile and happily responded, 'My name is Sara ...Sara Tanaka.'

'I'm glad to make your acquaintance.' He mockingly said, most formally, as he smiled back at her.

Adam then continued out to the waiting truck, threw his kit into the back, and climbed aboard before making his introductions to Chantel. As the truck pulled away, he looked back at Sara and winked and then smiled as she waved him off.

She was beaming and he thought, 'What a beautiful smile she really does have!'

Chantel was a happy and chatty young woman, but she did not have the striking good looks of Sara. Adam smiled to himself as he wondered if that is why Sara had chosen 'her' to give him a lift.

Chapter Three
Bus Station, Evans Mills,
New York State, USA

Chantel pulled up close to the Bus Station on Leray Street and they said their goodbyes as Adam jumped out and grabbed his gear from the back. The journey had taken only fifteen minutes. He slapped the side of the truck twice in rapid succession to confirm that he was done. Chantel then pulled out into the traffic and tooted her horn three times in salutation.

As the engine roared away Adam made his way into the building to wait for the next departure. Chantel inhaled deeply, breathing in the sandalwood aftershave that Adam wore, and which still filled the car. Then she let out a deep, longing sigh.

Adam took the bus to Syracuse where he changed and then headed to Buffalo on the Greyhound line. At Buffalo he had time for a meal in a local diner. It was basic but tasted great. He ate a large plate of chicken wings out of respect for the city as he always did whenever he passed through. There was something about the ubiquitous American diner that instantly gave him a great sense of comfort and familiarity. From there he left on the last and longest leg of his journey. Passing through Cincinnati he headed on to Louisville in Kentucky, close to the border with Indiana.

He was tired when he arrived and yet he still had nearly two hours until he reached his destination. Clintburg.

He checked the timetables and took a local bus to the outskirts of the city. From there he hitched the rest of the way. He was still in uniform, and he got lucky. Adam was twice picked up by ex-servicemen who did their best to accommodate him. The second driver was elderly and was happy to pass the time talking about his war stories. Adam found them very interesting, and it was happily distracting listening to the man recounting his exploits during his two tours in Vietnam.

He was a kindly soul, and he went out of his way to drop his traveller close to Clintburg. Far off on the horizon, it looked like storm clouds were gathering. He thought that with luck they would pass him by.

Adam walked the final two miles gathering his thoughts as he did so. The familiarity that he sensed as he closed on Clintburg gave him no comfort.

Chapter Four
Windy Pines Motel, Clintburg, Kentucky, USA

Light was fading as Adam walked onto the forecourt of the Windy Pines Motel. He knew it well from his childhood and it had hardly changed since then and had probably not changed much from when it was built in the 1940s.

To the front of the motel there was a small unkempt plant bed with an overly large flagpole and an American flag hanging lazily from it. Set amongst bedding plants was an electric sign, in brilliant blue with red lettering which screamed out, 'Entrance', on the top and 'Vacancy', on the bottom.

He had never known it to say, 'No Vacancy'.

The motel itself was arranged in a linear manner with rooms on two floors and a very dated metal staircase to the upper floor which had its own equally dated, overly ornate, metal railings. For the most part the building was white. Though the face of each room was roughly painted in a mix of turquoise blue and buttermilk yellow with the doors themselves being turquoise. The edge of the floor of the upper level was picked out in a rust red. It made for a truly striking colour scheme. In front of the building the tarmac had, once and long ago, been painted with lines for car parking spaces, though little of the paint remained. It mattered not, as the spaces were infrequently used.

At the end of the line of rooms furthest from Adam and closer to the town itself a flat roofed, single-storey office jutted out into the parking lot. It had windows on all three sides and unsurprisingly followed the same painting scheme as the rest of the building. The surrounding area was heavily wooded, but it was impossible to miss the motel as its presence was made evident by an excessively large neon sign above the office – 'Windy Pines Motel'.

Adam crossed the parking lot and made his way to the reception. As he entered, he passed a yucca plant that looked as if it had died, been brought back to life, and was then in the process of dying again. The room looked empty, as he slammed his hand down on the bell to call for attention. Pulling his hand away he could feel a layer of grime coming with it. He was acutely aware of the overpowering smell of stale smoke. Instantly a skinny, startled young man jumped up from the low seat which he had clearly been sleeping in, hidden as he was, behind the counter. The youth had several days of stubble and his greasy hair looked as if it had never seen a comb. He wore filthy dungarees and a T-shirt with holes in it – holes, that is, which were not meant to be there. As the clerk leant towards the counter the stench of stale body odour became overpowering. However, Adam's enhanced military training enabled his self-control to prevent him from retching.

'Uh ..., hi there...' he said sleepily, '...uh, yeah ...uh, well ...welcome to the Windy Pines Motel.'

The use of 'the' when referring to the Motel inferred a status which it most certainly did not have.

However, Adam responded, bowled over by the slick sales pitch, 'I'd like a room!'

'Right, uh ...how long for?'

'I'm not sure for now, but certainly three or four days at least.'

'OK, well in that case I can put you on our Goldstar Preferred Customer deal. That will be twenty-five bucks a night.'

The youth paused for a moment and then continued with a shifty look about him, 'Cash only!'

It crossed Adams mind that 'everyone' was offered the 'Goldstar deal'. Adam pulled out seventy-five dollars and laid it on the counter and he was handed a key with a plastic fob with the number fourteen on it. He noted that few of the other room keys were missing from the rack on the wall, where they would normally have hung. The lot was also almost devoid of vehicles.

He thought to himself, 'Not a great advert!'

As Adam went to leave the receptionist said, 'Hey, can I have your name and license plate number?'

'I've got no car, but my name is Adam Wolf.'

The young man had started lazily scribbling the details in a battered old diary. But on hearing Adam's name he did a doubletake. Adam didn't know the youth, but he certainly appeared to know, or know of, Adam.

As Adam left the office and walked along the front of the building towards his room the receptionist, thoughtfully, wrote in the diary, 'A. Wolf'.

Halfway across the lot, the sniper glanced back and saw the youngster furiously tapping the keypad of his phone before talking quickly into it. The youth struck Adam as a particularly sloth like individual, so Adam was surprised to note the speed with which he had made the call. Partway through the conversation the desk clerk turned and glanced out in Adam's direction. On seeing that Adam was staring at him he looked decidedly uncomfortable and turned away quickly before ending the call. As Adam opened the door of number fourteen the thought passed through his mind that he should have either haggled on the price or preferably gone elsewhere. The room smelt slightly damp and very musty. Having been in the military he had slept in worse places, though he couldn't remember when.

Adam was exhausted and lay on top of the bed falling asleep within a short time. He was awoken forty minutes later, by the sound of a car pulling up outside his room followed by a heavy knock on the door. Clearly, he was not expecting a visitor and Adam thought that it must be the receptionist who had come calling.

On opening, he saw the Sheriff - Carter. Adam remembered him from years before when the man had been a more junior officer, but he knew little of him. What he did know was that he was generally viewed as ineffectual, quick with his fists and arrogant. The officer was over six feet tall, balding, had a solid frame and a large belly. His strong unblinking eyes, Adam felt, lacked kindness.

'Adam, isn't it?' The law enforcement officer remarked.

'Yes.'

The Sheriff showed slight annoyance with the terse reply and Adam's tone, though he swiftly let it pass.

'I'm Sheriff Carter. I've just come to explain about the 'random murder' of your relatives.'

Adam thought it was a very peculiar way to start the conversation and to emphasis the supposedly 'random' deaths.

Since first being told in Afghanistan, Adam had presumed that his family had been murdered. However, he ignored the officer's words and asked, though he knew the answer to the question already, 'How did you know I was here?'

The Sheriff looked perturbed and stared back at Adam saying nothing for a moment, though his fists began to twitch.

He then responded emphatically, 'I know that this is a difficult time for you. I just wanted to let you know that we are doing everything we can to apprehend the perpetrators, but it seems to be clear that they are 'random killings', and it may prove difficult to catch the individuals.'

Noting the repeated use of 'random', Adam asked, 'How many 'random multiple killings' have occurred in this county in the last ten years?'

Carter said nothing, but a cold, aggressive look swept across his face. This, he could not easily hide. After a moment he replied in as conciliatory a tone as he could muster, 'I couldn't give you an exact number. I would have to go through the records.'

The law enforcement officer then recounted the manner of the family's death and his investigation thus far. Adam felt that he did so with relish.

Adam listened showing no emotion whatsoever.

'Thank you. If I need anything else from you, then I will be in touch.' Adam stated bluntly.

Carter's jaw dropped in surprise at Adam's tone, before Adam continued, 'In the meantime, once you've had a chance to check the number of 'random murders' then maybe you could let me know your findings?'

The officer looked as if a dark cloud had crossed his face. His hostile eyes bored into Adam's cold, rock-steady eyes.

'Look Adam, I understand that this is a traumatic time for you, but I have genuinely come here in friend-ship and to be of assistance.'

'Thank you, I have found this most illuminating.' Adam replied, in a voice that did not betray his inner thoughts.

Carter looked as though he was about to say some-thing, but before he could Adam shut the door while saying, 'Good night!'

Adam went back and lay on the bed. He could sense that Carter had not left his position at the door. How-ever, a few moments later he heard him slowly walk back to the patrol car. Adam listened as the Officer backed out and drove off. He heard the vehicle stop shortly after-wards for almost five minutes. The engine was left running. No doubt it had pulled up outside the motel office for that time, before finally leaving the premises.

Adam stared at the ceiling in the darkened room, un-able to sleep. He mulled the events over in his mind trying to draw conclusions from them. Eventually his body shut down and he drifted off into an unsatisfactory sleep.

Chapter Five
The Dirty Dollar Saloon, Clintburg, Kentucky, USA

The evening was drawing in and Adam slowly made his way along the highway to the edge of town. Long before he could see 'The Dirty Dollar Saloon' he became aware of the glow from the lights on the outside of the building which illuminated the parking area and the adjacent road.

Turning in towards the entrance, he saw that the gravelled area was almost full of an untidy assortment of trucks, station wagons, cars, and motorbikes in the parking lot. He also noticed the strong smell of alcohol on the breeze.

Adam could see that the bar hadn't changed since the last time he had drunk there with his brother, just prior to going on his first tour to Afghanistan. He felt a twinge of sadness pass over him as he remembered that happy night. Adam walked across the gravel and weaved his way between vehicles before climbing up a short flight of wooden steps. Hidden in the shadow of a truck on the opposite side of the road, a powerfully built man who had been following him looked on. He listened intently to the crunching sound of Adam's boots on the crushed rock. The man had an ugly scar above his right eye and an expressionless look on his face.

Adam could hear the busy chatter of the customers inside and the welcoming jukebox that was blaring out the song, 'Time for me to fly', by REO Speedwagon. As he opened the door a warm gust of stale beer and sweat swept over him whilst the intensity of the noise grew ever stronger. Several people glanced around as he entered the bar. Some of those who knew Adam by sight turned away with embarrassed glances whilst others gave a clenched smile of sympathy. Adam passed through the crowds nodding occasionally to certain individuals as he went.

A group of four out of town women in their mid-twenties followed his progress, giggling and chatting to each other furtively as they did so. As Adam passed them by, the only brunette in the group gave him a wide smile, briefly fluttered her eyelids, and said, 'Hi there!'

Adam smiled briefly and as he moved on, he replied plainly, 'Hello.'

Unseen by him, the girl turned to her friends,

shrugged her shoulders and then they burst out in laughter and rapid, secretive chatter. Adam squeezed his way through to the bar choosing the point nearest the only male bartender amongst three others.

On seeing the new customer, the man shouting out in recognition, 'Hey Adam!'

Adam nodded to him, calling loudly above the din, 'Hi Paul, how are you?'

Paul lent forward as Adam squeezed his way closer to the bar and Paul, furtively Adam thought, said, 'I'm real sorry about Danny and the family.'

'Thanks Paul!'

Adam continued, 'Would you like a Bud? It's on me!'

'Sure,' Paul retorted.

Adam was glad to see Paul again. They had both been on the football team at high school and had always been close friends. Paul was just under six feet tall, was black and muscular and he had a fine, handsome face with chiselled features. Adam smiled to himself when he remembered back to their high school days and the many girls who had tried to lure Paul with their charms.

Paul moved along the bar and pulled a long cold Budweiser until the froth gradually slipped down the side of the glass in currents. He came back and handed Adam the beer and as he did so, the sniper leant towards him and said in hushed tones, 'Paul I would like your help? I want to find out who did this?'

Paul came closer and was about to speak when Adam saw his eyes being drawn, momentarily, into the distance somewhere behind where the Marine stood.

Paul then said more loudly than necessary and with an air of nervousness, 'I'm sorry Adam, I don't know anything about what happened.'

As Paul moved away, Adam took a sip from the glass and then slowly rotated, leaning back against the bar as he did so. He carefully scanned the area and especially where Paul's gaze had been directed. He saw an unkempt individual standing, not far away and on his own. The guy tried to appear disinterested, but he was surreptitiously glancing at Adam. He tried to place the customer. Adam was sure that he knew him.

And then it came to him. The man had not aged well. Adam remembered him having been at his high school a few years below him. He had lank, greasy, badly combed hair which though dark, seemed to be going prematurely grey. The man's skin was sallow and heavily pockmarked though he covered it mostly with stubble of several day's growth. In the subtle lighting of the bar, he had a ghostly countenance with sharp, rat like features. He was about five feet, nine tall and was excessively thin. The man's clothes looked expensive though they were tasteless and on careful examination they also looked uncared for. The overall impression was shabby. He drank a cocktail which seemed incongruous among the other customers.

Adam had seen his type before, a low-level drug user and almost certainly a drug pusher as well. The sniper stared directly at the man who was unable to hold his gaze. Instead, he nervously turned away taking a sip from his glass as he did so.

Adam couldn't quite remember his name, Lloyd or Floyd, he seemed to remember. 'Yes Floyd!' He was sure of it.

While Adam was trying to assess Floyd, he felt a tap on his shoulder. He turned around to see Paul leaning over towards him with an outstretched arm. Again, Paul said in an excessively loud voice, 'Adam, I'm sorry but I forgot to give you your change.'

Adam looked at him thoughtfully and then glanced down at the clutch of dollar bills and coins that he had been passed. Strangely, he noticed writing on the top bill.

It read, 'I can't talk now! Meet me tomorrow morning at ten o'clock in the woods at the back of the Fire Department, P.'

Adam folded the top bill and handed it back to Paul ostensibly as a tip, winking as he did so. He then pocketed the rest of the cash and downed the remainder of the drink in one long gulp.

He turned suddenly and noticed that Floyd had been looking directly at him while his back was turned. Seeing the man's face again he thought to himself, 'Yes, Floyd – that's definitely it!'

Having his curiosity noted by Adam, he turned away rapidly. Adam pressed his way through the throng and past the group of girls once more. They all stopped talking and turned to smile at him, *en masse*. The girl who had spoken to him previously gently ran her hand through her hair as Adam, un-noticing, walked by.

Adam made his way to the door and, leaving, he descended the steps enjoying the bracing air of the evening. He couldn't help but wonder why Paul 'wanted to', or even 'had to' arrange a clandestine meeting.

Adam's solid rhythmic steps crunched through the gravel as he made his way back to the motel room. The touch of the fresh night air was very welcome after the stale overpowering smells of the bar. As he walked, he looked up into the night sky at the vast swathe of stars which filled the ink black sky, and it brought back thoughts of night patrols in the hills of Afghanistan.

Once the sniper had gone from the parking lot Floyd emerged stealthily from the bar. He crept down the steps and slithered across the gravel. Floyd then poked his head out into the road so that he had a view of Adam, who was by then some way off. He watched Adam until he had disappeared and then Floyd took out his cell phone and made a call. A few minutes later a battered old, brown Buick drove up and Floyd and the driver made off slowly in the same direction that Adam had taken.

Unseen and still in the trucks shadow, the watcher waited until the Buick was some way down the road before walking over to his own car.

He then followed Floyd.

Chapter Six
Windy Pines Motel, Clintburg, Kentucky, USA

Adam had woken early and after eating some of the complimentary biscuits that had been left on a side table, he had taken a long shower. It felt deeply relaxing. After getting dressed he sat on the bed while he contemplated. Adam then grabbed another biscuit. He wondered how many years they had lain there in their packet waiting for someone to risk eating one. He smiled as he thought, 'I'm glad I'm a Marine – I'm brave enough to do it!'

He laughed out loud as he considered, 'Anyway, you can't get hospitalised from eating stale cardboard!'

He had just tied his boot laces when he heard a rhythmic knock. He stopped smiling.

Expecting to see Carter or the desk clerk he opened the door with a mild sense of irritation.

'Hello Adam!' Kerri said in the sweetest of voices.

Adam stared at her transfixed.

His face softened and he broke into a wide smile saying, 'Hey Honey. It's great to see you again!'

He stepped aside and with his arm outstretched, he welcomed her in.

As she passed him by, he inhaled her intoxicating and familiar smell - a wild mix of perfume, hairspray, and exotic scented soaps.

Closing the door Adam said, 'Please sit down, Kerri.'

Rather than sit on the bed she crossed the room and sat on the only chair.

She was looking down at her hands when he shut the door and turned to her.

As she nervously rubbed the arm of the chair she said, 'I'm so sorry about what happened Adam.'

He looked into her eyes which were filled with emotion and with tears. They sparkled like newly cut diamonds, he thought to himself.

'I know you are.' He replied in the softest of voices.

He looked deep into Kerri's eyes and even deeper into his memories before he eventually said, 'I need your help.'

Then pausing he said, 'Do you know who did this?'

She sighed heavily, looked away and then said, 'Oh Adam! Please leave it alone. Danny would have wanted that!'

Inside Adam winced. He knew exactly what Danny would have wanted and it certainly would not have been to 'leave it alone'. Adam realized, however, that she said her words out of love and concern for him. He had no concern whatsoever, however, for himself.

'Please tell me everything that you know?' Adam sensitively questioned.

She looked at him and then burst into tears burying her head in her hands.

Kerri sobbed the words out to him, 'Adam... I... I... don't know much ...Well... not for sure!'

He knew in his very soul that it hadn't been 'random', but this confirmed his suspicions that there was more to this than Carter was letting on.

Kerri dried her eyes with her sleeve and tried to calm herself before saying, 'I have a friend in the Sheriff's department, and she told me that Danny came in a few weeks ago. He made a report about some drug dealers in the area. I asked Abigail what had been done about his complaint, but she told me that she didn't know, and things were a bit sensitive in there now, so she didn't want to ask questions.'

'Which officer did he speak to?'

Adam held his breath as he waited for a response.

Kerri looked furtive. Adam was certain that she was going to say Carter.

'Please Adam! I think that this will all ...just cause you trouble. Please don't ask me any more questions. I still love you Adam, you know that?'

He mellowed and said, 'I know you do Kerri. But this is something I *must* deal with. Who was it?'

She looked down at her hands and whispered, 'Chief Deputy Jervis Taylor.'

Adam was surprised, 'Isn't that Paul's uncle?'

Kerri looked worried as she slowly nodded, whispering, 'Please leave Adam! I don't want you to get ...'

Adam was stunned into silence.

He looked deep into Kerri's loving and imploring eyes. He wondered if those intoxicating eyes would also be grieving for him soon if he pushed on. But he knew that - push on, he must!

'Shall I drive you home Kerri?' Adam suddenly asked.

'Well, that was partly why I came over. I've brought my Mum's car. She rarely uses it now and she offered it to you while you are here.'

'Thank you, yes that would be a big help,' Adam replied, '...I could drop you home now if you like?'

Kerri stared into his strong, kindly eyes and she thought longingly to herself, 'No I don't like Adam!'

All she desired was to fall into his powerful arms, to feel his body warmth, and to stay there forever.

However, she wiped the tears away and whispered dejectedly, 'Yes, that would be lovely.'

Kerri got up to leave and took the keys from her bag, walking as she did so over to the door which Adam had just opened for her. As Kerri leant toward him placing the keys in his hand the sudden touch of his skin made her lose control. She pushed forward into his chest and slid her arms around him, her weeping face pressed into his strong chest.

She cried out, 'Oh Adam, I've never stopped loving you. I know it would never work out, but I couldn't bear losing you from my life forever. Please just go back to Afghanistan and forget this!'

He could feel the warm dampness of her tears leeching through his shirt and on to his skin. It made her love and her pain appear all the more real. He thought to himself that whatever lay in wait for him in Clintburg seemed much more dangerous than the Taliban in her view.

It was impossible for Adam not to be moved by her love and her concern for him, but his feelings for her were, as for one who was like a little sister to him. He looked down at her weeping face and consoled her, 'Kerri I will be O.K. I just need to sort a few things out and then I will head back to the Corps.'

He desperately wanted to tell her how much he loved her, though he did not wish to give her false hope.

'Come on, let's go for a drive. We will both feel better for it. You can show me your new home and I can meet Staci again. She must have grown up a great deal!'

Kerri gently pulled away and smiled through the tears as she thought about the joy of her life, Staci. 'Yes ...Yes, she has.'

Then looking into his warm face, she admitted, 'I should have known, after all these years, that there would be no stopping you, but I just had to try! If I can do anything to help you, then please ask me. Beware though, the last few years seem to have changed the character of the town we grew up in. There are quite a few unpleasant outsiders who have moved in and then there are the ones we always had.'

He smiled to her as she passed by heading for the car.

They climbed in and he slowly drove off, noticing that the youth in the office seemed to be very awake and very interested in them. Adam did not, however, notice the man with the scar above his eye who hid himself in his car at the far end of the parking lot.

Letting several minutes pass the watcher pulled out and followed Adam at a great distance.

Adam lowered his window and dropped his arm down the outside of the door, enjoying the cold breeze against his skin. It brought back very happy memories of when they were dating each other.

Chapter Seven
Fire Department, Clintburg, Kentucky, USA

Adam left Kerri's house at 9:45 a.m. and headed towards the Fire Station. The weather was turning, and a stiff breeze was beginning to blow. He lowered the window as he drove, enjoying the cool, blustery air in his face. Adam felt sorry for Kerri. The house was little more than a run-down shack and he had sensed that though she called it home, she felt ashamed of it.

It was a short drive and he pulled up a little way along the street from the Fire Department. There was nobody around, so he got out and walked towards it, turning down a dirt track to the side of the Station which led into the woods to the rear.

An ancient blue Chevvy was roughly pulled up part way down the track and Adam took this to be Paul's car. He passed by noticing that the doors were unlocked and that keys hung from the ignition. There was hardly any sound to be heard save for the sounds of nature.

Walking deeper into the trees he became aware of movement in among the densely packed trunks. In the distance he began to hear police sirens becoming more intense. Creeping forward more cautiously, he looked in horror at the scene before him.

Some thirty feet ahead of him he saw Paul. His body moved gently in the breeze in unison with the billowing branches and leaves.

As Adam ran forward - the blaring sirens and screeching tyres some way behind him were an irrelevance. Adam's heart was pounding as he jumped the fallen trunk of an ancient Chestnut oak which barred his way.

Reaching the small clearing where Paul's body hung by the neck from a black nylon rope, he lunged forward grabbing Paul's legs to lift his body. Unbeknown to him, Adam's effort to release the pressure was futile. Paul was already dead.

He looked up at Paul's lifeless face and clenched his eyelids shut to hide the scene from his view. Letting out a low moan, he exclaimed, 'Noooo!'

He heard running feet behind him and looking over his shoulder saw the Chief Deputy Sheriff and three Deputies racing towards him with their guns drawn. One of the junior officers was barking into his radio to someone at the other end, ordering an ambulance to be sent out urgently.

'Don't move!' Taylor's screeching his deeply emotional voice ordered.

The Chief Deputy Sheriff fired his gun twice into the trunk where the rope was tied off, severing the line as he did so with the second shot. Paul's upper body immediately dropped towards Adam and into the arms of two of the Deputies who had lunged forward to grab the lifeless, falling body. The third Deputy had stood back and levelled his pistol at Adam in case the suspect bolted or tried to attack them.

They laid the body down and Taylor ran forward pushing everyone away as he did so. He desperately gave his nephew the kiss of life for ten minutes before an ambulance crew arrived and pronounced the obvious. Paul was dead.

The Chief Deputy Sheriff, who struggled to control his horror and emotions, turned towards Adam with tears in his eyes. The Deputies who had watched the pathetic and sad attempt of their boss trying to save his kin, now turned towards Adam. They, and the senior officer who slowly rose from his knees, stared at Adam, none with more hatred in his eyes than Chief Deputy Sheriff Taylor.

Taylor drew his handgun which he had previously re-holstered and levelled it at Adam.

One of the officers stepped forward to save Taylor from his own actions, growling at Adam as he pointed his revolver at the suspect, 'Don't move. You are under arrest. Turn around nice and slow and put your hands behind your head and interlock your fingers.'

Clearly unhappy with the aggressive look that Adam returned to him, coupled with a lack of any movement, the Deputy screamed, 'Now!'

As Adam complied the other Deputies also drew their weapons and kept him covered as the first officer barked, 'Turn around!'

Adam slowly turned while the officer purposely moved forward holstering his weapon and drawing the handcuffs from his belt as he did so. As he handcuffed Adam he continued, 'You are under arrest for murder!'

The Deputy grabbed his upper arm before leading him back down the track. It was clear to Adam that he was being framed, as he wondered, 'But why? And by whom?'

Adam was led along the line of Police Patrol Vehicles to a mud-spattered Chevrolet Tahoe. As he was roughly pushed into the back of the PPV, Adam looked over at the Chief Deputy Sheriff who glared at him from a short distance away with a face filled with pure venom. Taylor had the look of a fanatic, hell-bent on murder!

The strong smell of antiseptic in the vehicle was testament to the clean the vehicle had undergone the night before when a troublesome drunk had been arrested. He had promptly and violently vomited inside the PPV. The odour helped to clear Adam's mind while he focused on his situation.

As the vehicle drove away, he could see the paramedics loading Paul's body into the back of the ambulance.

'What a waste!' he thought.

Chapter Eight
Sheriff's Department, Clintburg,
Kentucky, USA

Adam was brought into the station and the desk sergeant processed him. He was fingerprinted and the contents of his pockets were removed, as were his belt and laces.

The sergeant then stated in a monotone voice, 'You have the right to remain silent. Anything you say, can and will be used against you in a court of law. You have the right to an attorney. If you cannot afford an attorney, one will be provided for you. Do you understand the rights I have just read to you? With these rights in mind, do you wish to speak to me?'

Once the Miranda rights had been given to Adam he replied only to say, 'I do not require an attorney.'

Then he was silent.

One of the deputies then placed the sniper in a holding cell.

After several hours Adam was passed a plate of food

and a cup of water through a slot in the door, by a young female officer who eyed him cautiously. Adam looked at her and thought that there was more than a hint of sadness about the woman. He also felt that she looked hostile towards him. Adam noticed her name on a metal name tag just above her shirt pocket said, 'T. Lawson.'

The food he had been given was plain, but good and the chocolate dessert had tasted quite pleasant. After eating he lay on the bed, trying to make sense of what had occurred.

Just before 4:00 p.m. two deputies came for him and led him through to the interview room. As indicated to him, Adam sat down on a small wooden chair on the far side of a grey metal table. The officers said nothing as they retired from the room. Moments later the door opened, and Adam stared into the expressionless eyes of the Chief Deputy Sheriff. Statuesque, Taylor stood staring straight at Adam, before closing the door behind him.

Scraping the second chair away from the table he sat down sinking into it as a man who had the troubles of the world on his shoulders. As he did so, the door opened again and in walked Deputy T. Lawson. She said nothing, though Taylor acknowledged her presence with a quick glance. Rather than sit beside Taylor in the vacant chair she moved to the corner and stood observing the interview.

'I'm Chief Deputy Sheriff Taylor. I will be asking you some questions.'

He sighed before continuing, 'I was informed that you have been read your rights, so I know that you know that you do not have to answer. I understand that you do not require an attorney?'

Taylor looked at Adam in expectation of an answer, but none came so he continued, 'Why did you kill...' he gulped, '...Paul?'

Adam looked into his eyes, incredulously. 'Paul was my friend! I didn't kill him!'

The officer started, 'We found you...'

Adam cut him short and snaped back at him, 'How did you arrive so quickly?'

Irritated by the interruption the Chief Deputy Sheriff sneered at him, 'We received an anonymous tip off!'

'Anonymous!' Adam stifled a laugh and then replied calmly. 'Surely you can see that I am being framed!'

Taylor appeared to ignore Adam's words asking, 'How did you lure ...Paul to that location?'

'I did not 'lure' him!' Adam replied strongly, continuing, 'I hadn't seen Paul for over a year before yesterday. I spoke to him at the Dirty Dollar last night.'

Taylor paused for a moment, as if he was trying to fathom the unfathomable.

The natural break gave Adam time to consider the turn of events. He pondered whether it was appropriate for the victim's uncle to interview a suspect. Adam smiled inwardly as he thought that a lawyer would have a field day with that in court. It had crossed his mind, however, that Taylor had no intention of letting Adam make it to court!

He stopped smiling.

The Chief Deputy suddenly said, 'What did you speak about?'

'I wanted to know if he had any information about who had killed my brother and his family. Paul didn't want to talk to me then. He seemed nervous. He asked me to meet him this morning behind the Fire Department. I arrived just before you did. He was already hanging there. I tried to save him, but...'

The officer glanced away, wincing as he did so.

Taylor looked exhausted. He turned back to Adam and said, 'Is there anything else that you wish to say in your defence?'

Adam thought momentarily before saying, 'I left Kerri's house shortly before I found Paul. She will be able to verify this. It would not have given me enough time to kill Paul in that manner.'

Adam stared at the man seeing the pain in his face and then continued, 'Paul knew something. I am sure of that. He was scared! He wrote a note on a dollar bill arranging the meeting...'

Taylor looked surprised, as he unbelievingly barked, 'Where is the note?'

'I gave it back to Paul as a tip.'

'Keep him here!' Taylor ordered, as he turned to Lawson before abruptly leaving the room.

Adam considered whether he should mention Floyd. He decided not to. He would like to deal with Floyd himself and he did not know if Taylor was trustworthy. He was clearly distressed at the death of his nephew, but that did not mean that he was not a part of any wrongdoing that was going on.

The Chief Deputy Sheriff went into the main office saying to no one in particular, 'Where are the contents of the ...the ...deceased's pockets.'

A young female officer jumped up from her desk and walked over to him with a shallow open topped brown box. She had been typing up an inventory of its contents.

Taylor fingered through the items. He noted that there was a mobile phone, a half empty packet of bubble gum – very sticky, a few coins, along with several banknotes. The notes were a ten-dollar bill, three five dollars and six single dollars. He picked up the one-dollar bills and passed them through his hands as he turned and examined them. The fourth dollar he looked at did indeed have the message that Adam had spoken of. Taylor stared into the middle-distance and pondered. He knew that his officers had interviewed the Fire Chief and the Firefighters who had been on duty at the station. They had heard a car go down the track an hour before any law enforcement vehicles had arrived. It had not come back out. They also confirmed that a second car had arrived 'just' prior to the Deputies turning up. One of the fire crew had gone to the store and had seen it park up, before a man got out and went down the track on foot.

Taylor thought for a moment, grinding his teeth as he did so.

'That must have been Adam!' he mused.

'Deputy 'T'. Lawson!' Adam said as he stretched and lean back in his chair in the interview room.

He smiled at the officer who stood in the corner, and he slowly continued, 'I wonder what 'T' stands for?'

Waiting for a response he passed his hand slowly across the table-top sensing the smoothness against his skin. He noted that she did not return his smile, preferring to stay silent with a cruel sneer written harsh across her face. Then, suddenly, thoughtful, she forced a smile and said, 'Tina!'

'That's a sweet name ...Deputy.' He responded, smiling once more.

She said nothing but seemed to soften her face regardless. He looked at her and saw that same sadness he had noticed before.

'Is something troubling you?' he questioned sympathetically and without expecting an answer.

A dark cloud seemed to cross her face and as Tina glanced away, she looked tearful.

Then she turned back to Adam and said, 'My

boyfriend has been murdered! Does that count as some-thing troubling me!'

Adam was momentarily stunned. Then he slowly said, 'Who was your boyfriend?'

She looked thoughtful, was silent for a time and then stuttered in response, 'Paul ...Paul!'

And then, more emphatically, 'It was Paul!'

She suddenly broke down in tears.

He considered what she had told him before saying, 'But Paul never mentioned any girlfriend?'

Again, she looked thoughtful before saying, 'Why would he! He was black and I am white. His uncle was my boss!'

She paused before stuttering, 'You know how un-pleasant some people can be. We ...we ...thought it best ... to keep it secret!'

She thought back to happier times with her boyfriend as tears ran down her face and dreamily, she said, 'I loved him, despite what people thought of him! And now he is gone because of your family!'

'Tina – I swear to you that I did not kill him! He was my friend. Surely, he told you that! Why would I have harmed him? I tried to save him – whatever it looks like!'

While Adam sat waiting for Taylor to return, he won-dered why Tina had said of Paul, '...despite what people thought of him! ...'

Adam had known Paul for most of his life and he

knew of nobody who had a bad word to say of him. Certainly, Paul had always been well liked and popular! Adam wondered if there was something that he didn't know about his dead friend.

In the main office Taylor next sent two officers to interview Kerri and they radioed back to say that she did indeed verify Adam's account.

Jervis stood looking out of the window at nothing in particular, the crumpled dollar bill held tightly in his hand. The Chief Deputy Sheriff considered what he knew and came to certain vague conclusions.

He knew that Paul was a childhood friend of Adams. Though he also accepted that their friendship did not negate the possibility that Adam had murdered him. Maybe something in their shared past had led Wolf to kill his nephew. The anonymous tip-off did seem suspicious, swift, and opportune. The dollar bill, the Fire crew and Kerri all verified Adam's account.

However, most telling was that despite Adam hearing the police sirens from quite a distance away he had not made ` a run for it and had in fact 'appeared' to be trying to support Paul's body rather than pulling down on his legs to ensure that he died. Taylor did consider that possibly Adam was too late to escape, so he made sure Paul was dead and then gave the appearance of trying to save him.

The Chief Deputies eyes suddenly looked shifty. One item from the crime scene had not been placed in the evidence box by Jervis Taylor. An omission that Jervis had never made before and an omission which pained him.

The Chief Deputy Sheriff had searched the scene himself. Clenched in Paul's hand he had found a crumpled note which purported to be his confession in relation to the murder of Adams family. It was clear evidence against Paul. It also indicated an obvious motive firmly implicating Adam in Paul's murder. The note was typed which, in itself, was suspicious. If Paul had committed suicide, which the note 'could' be seen to indicate, then the officer would have expected it to be handwritten by the 'supposedly' troubled mind of the deceased and certainly not typed. Taylor had concerns about the document's authenticity, especially as it mentioned the other perpetrators. The Chief Deputy Sheriff knew Jeb, Buck, and Wade, and he remembered that Paul had always disliked them. He also disbelieved the last sentence of the note which further admitted that Paul had killed the others and dumped their bodies in a disused quarry. In a crudely clever touch, it ended asking for forgiveness from Adam.

Taylor walked back to the brown evidence box which lay alone on a desk, dropped the dollar bill from his hand and watched it float down to join its comrades.

He turned to the female officer and said without looking at her, 'Release the suspect!'

She looked surprised, as did other officers in the room, but she complied immediately.

As she walked towards the interview room Taylor continued cryptically under his breath, '...for the time being!'

Chapter Nine
Sleepy Hollow Cemetery, Clintburg, Kentucky, USA

Adam's brother had not been particularly religious, though his wife had been a devout Baptist. The children had also been brought up in the Baptist religion. Danny had, for the most part gone to Church with them out of respect for his wife.

Adam visited the Church and had spoken to the Pastor. He was a kindly old man who was clearly shocked and horrified by what had happened. The Pastor was also deeply concerned for Adam, and he had offered to speak with him at length if he felt that it would help him the Marine his grief.

Adam had been profoundly touched by the kindness and humanity of the Pastor, but he replied, 'I'm sincerely grateful for your offer, but my grief is the fuel which I must now let burn, as it will propel me on my journey.'

The Pastor tried to make sense of Adam's mystifying response. But the conclusion he kept returning to was, that Adam's journey would not be a happy one.

The Pastor, Larry Warren, offered to make the funeral arrangements on behalf of Adam's brother's family. He explained that they had been active members of the church and that they had done a great deal to aid it, and he felt a deep sense of personal loss.

Adam contacted friends and family who he felt might wish to attend, though he himself was estranged from many of them. On the day of the funeral and as the four coffins arrived at the Church a Sheriff's Department PPV slowly pulled into the carpark and the uniformed Sheriff stepped out. Adam noted that he had not been invited. The coffins passed through the front door as Adam watched, showing no emotion. The mourners walked in but as Carter neared the door, Adam, in full dress uniform stepped in front of him and said in a steely voice, 'This is a private ceremony.'

It had been said within earshot of some of the mourners and the Sheriff's face flushed purple in anger.

However, he maintained his composure with great difficulty and then turned back to his Ford Taurus saying, 'As you wish!'

As Carter climbed into his vehicle he looked back at Adam. He was gripped with a violent rage as he glared at the Marine.

Adam looked out across the surrounding countryside and saw in the distance, dark clouds gathering, accompanied by the low rumble of thunder. He could smell change in the air and could feel a cold breeze brush his face.

The cruelty of the families' deaths and the young children's loss, in particular, did make for a very emotional scene. However, overall, the ceremony passed by much as any such sad ceremony would.

Kerri came up to Adam at the end of the service, tears running down her face, and she said, 'Adam I'm so desperately sorry for you and your family. It has really scared a lot of us in the community!'

He couldn't say anything in reply. Though he held his composure, he felt as though his heart had been ripped out, all the more so, when he viewed the little children's coffins.

The four hearses left the Church and slowly headed for the Sleepy Hollow Cemetery on the outskirts of town. They were followed by a long procession of cars. Many of its graves harked back to the early days of Clintburg, nearly two-hundred years before. Since then, it had gradually grown, along with the history of the town. On a low rise to the eastern side of the Cemetery a deep double grave had been dug. During the drive to the Cemetery a light, mist-like, rain had begun to fall. By the time the mourners had arrived at the graveside, the rain was heavy and consistent. Adam looked at the piles of excavated soil with its muddy rivulets running down the face and disappearing into the grass at their base. Looking at the mourners the rows of closely packed umbrellas reminded him of the Testudo formation used by the ancient Romans. A stiff breeze was blowing, but the mourners were given some further protection by a nearby group of three mature Black Gum trees. The vast trees stood tall and animated against the darkening sky.

Adam's former girlfriend and her daughter had stood beside him as the Pastor said his last prayers and the caskets were laid to rest together. Seeing the coffins descending into the rich, reddish-brown Kentucky soil, Adam, unseen by the other mourners, was utterly consumed by a cruel sense of loss and a yearning to get hold of those who were responsible. The mourners gradually drifted away, with many of the women and some of the men weeping as they departed. Kerri and her daughter had remained after the burial, though feeling that he would like some time on his own they had walked back towards the car to wait for him.

Adam looked down at the pathetic sight of the four coffins and for the first time, tears began to roll down his face. He wished that he had, at that point, a better sense of his inner Faith. He recited the prayers that he had been taught as a child and that he had not spoken for many years. Then he crouched down and grabbed a handful of the damp soil. Standing, he cast his arm out across the coffins seeing the dirt fall in a wide arc. The rat-tat-tat, as it hit the coffin lids pounded on his very soul. He looked up at the dark skies through the dancing leaves of the Black Gums and as he did so, rain washed away his tears.

He then looked down into the grave and said, 'I was not here to protect you, but I am here now, and I will do my duty! Rest softly my lovelies.'

The wind abated momentarily and then made a slight turn in direction. As it did so the faintest scent of wild-flowers was discernible, and in a way, a floral tribute to the recently deceased.

He then came to attention and saluted. He was watched by his old girlfriend and her child, the Sheriff and two gravediggers who stood waiting at a respectful distance away on the far side of the trees.

Unseen by Adam, he was also being watched by Floyd who was hiding behind an ornate tombstone which had begun to lean severely, over the years, and which dated from 1857. Floyd smiled smugly to himself, feeling that he had some sort of power over Adam and that he was intruding, unwanted, into his deeply private affairs.

Unknown by that poor unfortunate, he in turn was being watched by another set of attentive and curious eyes, which peered out of the shadows amid a thicket of sugar maples. The trees grew wild on the far side of the cemetery wall. One of the eyes had a deep scar above it. The watchers rough, calloused fingers on his right hand traced the path of the scar as his thoughts percolated.

The eyes which watched were hostile.

Chapter Ten
Windy Pines Motel, Clintburg, Kentucky, USA

It had been a stormy night with intermittent thunder and lightning, away on the horizon. Adam had not slept well and had been troubled by happy memories from years before and a mind that wrestled to understand what was going on. He wondered if he would ever recover from this horrendous blow.

He got dressed at 5:00 a.m. and went out for a long walk along the highway before following a track up through the forest. The only sounds that he heard were of an occasional owl and the more general chatter of songbirds. Coming to the brow of a hill, set deep within the trees, he looked down on a long shallow valley with a small river running through it. He stopped for a moment taking in the view in the chill morning air. He could hear the gently bubbling waters far below as they echoed up through the forest. Momentarily he felt a sense of peace, but as soon as it came, it was gone again.

The rains from the night before had made the going more difficult and the clay-like soil clung tenaciously to his boots. He looked down at them and noted that his jeans were also heavily mud spattered.

Suddenly, over to his right he heard a twig break. Instinctively, he silently dropped to a crouch and noticed movement approximately seventy yards away. A few moments passed before his mood lightened and he began to smile to himself, slowly resuming his full height as he did so. Looking past the swathe of trunks, he caught sight of a majestic white-tailed deer. She was an adult and was slowly meandering through the forest eating beech and hickory nuts which had fallen from nearby trees.

He stood transfixed by the beauty of nature. He became aware of several other deer moving along at the same pace, but deeper into the forest.

Then suddenly spooked by something unseen the deer darted off effortlessly through the trees and into obscurity. As Adam stared after the creature, smells of decay and new life, bursting from the forest floor, filled his nostrils.

Adam scanned the area but saw nothing untoward and then decided to turn and walk back towards the motel. He could not say why, but he had some inner sense which told him that he was being watched, though he saw no sign of anyone.

The deer had indeed been frightened, not by any sight and not by any sound. But they had picked up a faint scent on the wind. It was a smell that they knew very well, and it meant danger. It was the scent of a human. It was not Adam's scent.

Watching Adam from far away amidst a thicket, the man with the scar above his eye crouched motionless. He did not move for a considerable time, preferring to let Adam disappear into the distance. When he did proceed, he did so cautiously, and he took a wide detour around the route that Adam had taken. However, the path that he took followed the same general direction.

Adam grabbed breakfast in a Denny's diner along the way. He feasted on a large plate of pancakes, maple syrup, orange juice and several cups of black coffee. It was his favourite choice whenever he went to Denny's and had been since childhood. The constituents and the flavours brought back particular moments in time with his family. Very ordinary times, but so very important to him. Adam ate slowly using the meal as a form of therapy ...drifting away to another world. A happier world.

Paying the check, he headed back to the motel.

He flicked through the tatty, old phone directory in his room and made a telephone call to the Jefferson County Coroner's office in Louisville. As he listened to the tone, he could feel the layer of grease and dirt on his fingers which he had picked up from the pages he had turned. The young woman who answered the phone sang out in quite a musical tone, 'Coroner's office how can I help?'

'Is the Coroner in today ...that is, all day?' Adam enquired as he rubbed his fingers clean on his trouser leg.

'May I ask who's calling?' She cautiously responded.

Adam lied, 'I'm calling from FedEx, and we have a delivery that has to be signed for personally by the coroner.'

'Yes, she is in today, but she may well leave soon after 5:30 p.m.'

Adam said, 'Thank you, I will tell the driver.'

He gently replaced the receiver. He did not want to give the coroner advance notice that he was coming, but he did want to make sure that she was there.

Adam showered. The smell of the exotic oil scented shampoo brought back thoughts of central-south Asia, and another life far away! The cool water which cascaded slowly down his body did not remind him of that region, except possibly the constant sense of thirst. He got dressed, before leaving the room and driving off towards Louisville. It was an uneventful journey which allowed him time to collect his thoughts.

Chapter Eleven
Coroner's Office, La Grange Rd, Louisville, Kentucky, USA

The Coroner's Office was in the Central State Hospital, and he left his car in the adjacent car park. He followed the signs and on arriving he asked the receptionist, 'Can I speak to the coroner?'

'Have you got an appointment?' the young woman asked as she flicked through the coroner's appointments diary.

'No, but I have come about my family ...my brother and his family were killed recently.'

The receptionist looked slightly unnerved as she knew who the man was talking about. She also recognised the sound of his voice from the earlier telephone call.

'I'm afraid the coroner is busy and ...and you must have an appointment to ...to see her.'

Adam was silent for a moment before saying, 'I would be grateful if you could ask, if she would see me 'now'. I don't have a great deal of time as I'm just back on leave from overseas and I must return soon.'

The woman looked about nervously and then said, 'Please wait here for a moment.'

Then she said, 'Can I just take your name please?'

'Adam.'

She walked over to a white, wooden door and knocked once, and without waiting for an answer, she entered. As the receptionist shut the door behind her, she glanced back surreptitiously at Adam. As the door closed, he looked at the sign at the top. It read, Gemma Carter MD. Coroner.

Moments later the young woman re-opened the door saying happily, 'Please come through Adam.'

As he entered, the receptionist disappeared out through the door and shut it behind her. He noticed that she had given him a quizzical look as she went.

The coroner was sat behind a large, ornate, wooden desk which was covered in crime scene photographs, toxicology reports and various case papers. She stood up as Adam came in and she said, 'Please take a seat. I am deeply sorry about what happened to your family Adam. It has been very distressing for the whole community, and I can only imagine what it has been like for you.'

Adam said nothing as he sat down, before the coroner continued sympathetically, 'Please call me Gemma. How can I help you?'

'I've got some questions about what happened ...to them.' Adam asked.

The coroner replied rather officiously, 'Surely the police are keeping you informed? I'm not sure that it would be proper for me to speak to you without their knowledge.'

As she said this, he felt that there was an imperceptible change in her face. Adam said, 'I have received 'some' information from them, Gemma, but I felt that you may well be more ...forthcoming.'

The coroner looked at him inquisitively and was silent for a moment. Then, looking downcast, she let out a long, slow response, 'Yeeesss!'

She changed the topic, 'I understand that you are on deployment abroad. May I ask what your role is?'

Adam presumed that she had gained this indication from her assistant. He was, in some respects, happy to take his mind away from the business in hand and back to where he felt more comfortable, with thoughts of his comrades.

'I'm a sniper,' then he paused and continued, '...in the Marines.'

Reproachfully she barked, 'I understand that you also moonlight as a FedEx driver!'

Adam looked non-plussed and allowed his lips to turn up in the merest of embarrassed responses.

Pausing momentarily, she then broke into the prettiest of smiles and chuckled to herself. Her lips were set off in a brilliant Dior Rouge lipstick which contrasted captivatingly with her sparkling white teeth.

She continued generously, 'No need to answer – I am sure that it is related to some sort of covert op!'

Adam couldn't help but feel drawn to her through the warmth of her personality.

Gemma mused, 'My father was a Marine. He served in Vietnam. It was a long time ago now, but once a Marine always a Marine or so he says!'

She was thoughtful and then said, 'He was never the same after his time in the Corps.'

Adam enquired, 'Is he still alive?'

'Yes ...yes, he is thankfully. He lives on Long Island and spends his days writing about his experience's 'up country', taking shade under a large plum tree whilst my mom bakes.'

Adam noted that she looked wistful and that her eyes were imperceptibly moist.

She smiled at Adam thoughtfully and then continued, 'Because of him, I've always had a soft spot for the military and in particular the Marines. Okay I'll help you, but on one condition!'

'What's that?'

'I ask that what I say to you remains between us and that you do not mention to the Sheriff's Department that we have spoken.'

Her response served to further prove an impression of

the Law Enforcement Agency, or at least some of its officers, that had already begun to form in his mind.

'That's fine by me!' Adam said.

'Right then, well fire away.' The coroner requested.

He looked at the middle-aged woman before him and thought how pretty she was for her age and surprisingly jolly given the, as some would see it, macabre career that she had chosen. 'Maybe her inner cheeriness was what kept her sane.' he thought.

As Adam began to speak, the coroner stepped back behind her desk and sat gently into the chair.

'Some of these questions may prove difficult for you to answer.' He said generously.

'I know the matter very well Adam, I will do my best to assist you.'

Adam paused thoughtfully and continued, 'The Sheriff has given me the impression that these were just ...' Adam said, sighing as he continued, '...random killings and that it is unlikely that they will find the perpetrators. May I have your views on that?'

Gemma glanced down at the floor momentarily and then looked directly at Adam saying, 'The Sheriff's Department may have their own reasons for coming to that conclusion and I cannot comment on that.'

She broke off, turned, and looked out through the window for a moment and then spun back towards Adam before continuing, 'The truth is Adam I'm not a detective. I can only make my judgements from what I see. However, that said, I find 'their' conclusions troubling. From what I know of the case and from my own work it appears to me that your brother's family was specifically targeted by at least three or four individuals. I suspect from what I've seen that your brother was the main target. Whoever did this wished to cause him maximum mental anguish and physical pain. I believe that it was personal and that the deceased ...your brother, may well have known the killers.'

Adam's hands gripped the arms of the chair so tightly that if they had not been made of metal, then they would probably have broken away.

His knuckles were pure white as he continued, 'Why do you say that?'

Gemma considered her thoughts for a moment before she spoke. 'I do not wish to distress you Adam, so I will try to put things in as clear and sensitive a way as possible. However, I feel that it is important that you are given the true facts. Your brother had been shot and beaten prior to his death. But rather than leaving it at that or simply killing him at that point, the perpetrators tied him to a chair. They then made him watch as they killed his children in front of him and repeatedly brutalised his wife. Her heart gave out due to the traumatic attack. Again, rather than kill your brother then, they left him tied to the chair as they proceeded to burn the house down while he was still alive. During my discussions with the investigators, it appears that nothing obvious was missing from the house. Judging by my own experience, this has all the hallmarks of a gang or revenge attack.'

Adam stared into her eyes emotionless - he was unable to speak to her momentarily. She was understanding and had a gentle way with her, and she just waited to give him time to collect his thoughts.

'Gemma, can I ask if you know of any other apparently 'random' killings which have occurred in this area over the last say ten or twenty years?'

'I thought that you might ask that. No, Adam.' She replied before saying immediately, 'I cannot. Killings in this area are mostly related to domestic violence and the occasional killing of a suspect by a police officer in furtherance of his or her duty.'

She was silent for a moment, 'I should clarify this though. 'I' do not feel that there have been other 'random' killings, however, there has been one other incident just over a year ago which bears a very strong resemblance to this one. The police concluded, in those killings, that the matter was 'random'. The case was closed without finding the killers. I did not agree with their findings.'

'Can you tell me the facts of that matter?' Adam enquired.

She sat forward in her chair and placed her arms on the desk saying, 'Yes. It was almost a mirror image of what occurred here. A young man - I believe that he had just turned twenty, was tied up in his house and was forced to watch as his father was killed in front of him. Then his mother and sister were both bound up and savagely brutalised before being shot. The young man was left tied up, as the perpetrators burnt the house to the ground.'

'How could the Sheriff conclude that one or both ... sets of killings could possibly be 'random' and unconnected?'

Gemma slowly sat back in her chair and then replied slowly, 'Exactly!'

'Thank you for your time, Gemma. You've been so very considerate and helpful.'

'Adam, I am trying to bring my concerns about what is going on to the attention of higher authorities, but I seem to be stonewalled so far. I will keep pressing!'

Adam stood up and shook her hand, as she also rose. The coroner walked over to the door and grasped the handle to open it for him. But she let the door remain shut.

Gemma placed her free hand gently on Adam's arm and whispered, 'Adam please be careful. Something is very wrong over there!'

The warmth of her hand was comforting. The smell

of the Red Door perfume by Elizabeth Arden which she wore, smelt deeply feminine and alluring.

He smiled at her, as she opened the door for him to leave, saying only, 'Roger that!'

As Adam walked back to his car, he was only too aware of the difficulties and the dangers that he faced. She was not the first person to warn him!

Chapter Twelve
The Harrison Brothers Quarry, outskirts of Clintburg, Kentucky, USA

It was 11:00 a.m. when the receptionist at the Sheriff's Department took the call. It had been a quiet morning up to that point, but things were about to change.

It was a cloudy day, but there was no forecast for rain. As they often did, the three young McGuiness brothers had gone fishing to a local quarry which had flooded many years before. They knew the quarry very well because it was their favourite spot for catfish and bass. Though it had been a hive of activity when the quarry was in use, it had long since been shut down and other more fruitful quarries opened in its place. The boys got on well together and they were never happier than when they were sat by the remote quarries edge trying to catch fish.

The moment they had arrived the boys felt that something was wrong. Looking across the dark water to the far side they could see the dense scrub surrounding the edge of the cliff had been crushed. Some of it lay desperately hanging by woody sinews against the stark quarry wall. The violent opening in the expanse of green was the size of a vehicle and when they looked across the still water, they could see an oil slick on the far side like a shimmering pancake. They were scared and, in unison, they ran home straight away. It was their parents who decided to make the call. They were sure that the story the children had told was true because the boys looked so shaken up.

Ten minutes later a Ford Explorer Utility Police Interceptor pulled up outside their home. The Deputy asked the father and his eldest son to come with him to show him exactly where the quarry was located. The officer knew of the recent horrific events at Adams brothers house, and he wondered if this new report may well be connected. Thirty minutes later the Deputy placed a call through to the office and explained that he believed that a truck or van had been pushed into the quarry and judging by the damaged undergrowth it appeared as if this had been done relatively recently. He explained that they would need an underwater team as the quarry was deep and its waters were murky.

The Deputy continued to look around as the father and son left on their short walk home. There was a strong smell about the quarry of oil and fuel. The place was eerily quiet, and he had a sense of foreboding. Like some of the other officers and townsfolk he had a heightened sense of concern given the unusual and troubling events which had befallen the town over the last few years.

He went back to his vehicle and sat in the driver's seat waiting for the other officers to attend. The smell of disinfectant in the vehicle and the touch of the steering wheel which he nervously played with gave him some comfort.

He didn't have long to wait.

Chapter Thirteen
Road through forest, near Clintburg,
Kentucky, USA

Adam had seen the increasing traffic through and out of Clintburg - police patrol vehicles, fire trucks and ambulances, many with sirens blazing ...and the ghouls, desperate to see the crime scene and to be pictured in the background on the news. He had also heard tell of a specialist underwater team which had been drafted in. Adam had casually made enquiries of the locals whom he had met when he was in town, and they explained that a truck had gone into the old Harrison brother's quarry and that police believed there were several bodies down there. Some of the locals even hinted at who may have died. They had worked it out from the description of the vehicle and the rumours around town about three troublesome, local youths who had recently gone missing.

It did cross Adams mind that if he bumped into the Sheriff again that Carter might, once more, suggest that they were just 'random' killings. He headed back to the motel and picked up his car before heading out to the quarry. Rather than trying to drive straight down to the quarry he pulled into a small clearing some way from the turnoff and parked his car. He then headed across country. It was easy going as the mature trees kept much of the light from the forest floor which suppressed most of the undergrowth.

As he came close to the spot, he heard a great deal of noise with people shouting, cars and trucks revving and machinery in operation. He was still relatively high up and he crept towards the quarry's edge hidden from view behind a dense, red chokeberry shrub. He peered across the cliff wall to the far side of the quarry which lay lower down as the quarry had originally been cut into a slope. Adam could see police tape cordoning off the area around the gaping hole in the brush. Branches and bushes still hung by their torn fibres and roots, where they had been violently ripped from their slumber.

Many officers were milling around, and one person was taking photographs of the scene down near the water's edge where the nearby crane was running on idle. The long grasses which helped to hide Adam gently brushed his face as a light breeze blew across the scene. He could see the recovered truck covered in weed and dead branches standing motionless and close-by the quarry edge. One of the doors was half open and the front end was coated in thick mud. Water was still dripping from the vehicle into a great pool beneath it, which effortlessly trickled its way back into the quarry.

One body bag was being loaded into an ambulance whilst another corpse was being placed into a bag behind a screen used to shield the team from the large crowd which had gathered to watch. Nearby the third body, Wade, lay, ugly and lifeless on the dirt. His face was badly disfigured from the blow it had taken when Floyd had violently struck him with the rock. Piles of smaller rocks lay in the pool of water around the body where they had tumbled from his overstuffed pockets. The photographer had begun to take shots of the body from every angle imaginable. He kept his distance though as an ugly smell had begun to emanate from the body as the day warmed up.

Adam crept down the slope and gradually mingled into the crowd. They were quite excited by the events and were animated in their views as to what had occurred. He recognised some onlookers, but many he had never seen before. The ghoulish activity clearly fascinated people, some of whom had come from quite a substantial distance away. Adam casually questioned individuals as he encountered them. From what they had overheard directly or had learnt through gossip they said that three males were found at the bottom of the quarry along with a truck. It seemed that the vehicle had been pushed in after the deceased had been thrown into the water.

Everyone in the crowd seemed to agree that the three men had been murdered. An occasional person suggested, in whispered tones, the probable names of the dead. The same three names kept being repeated. When asked why they could possibly have been murdered nobody wished to say, though it was clear to Adam that they did have views on the subject. However, the more he probed the topic, the more suspicious they became, before clamming up.

Adam noticed that he was increasingly becoming a person of interest for some members of the crowd. One heavily, bearded man in greasy overalls, who had a serious body odour issue, became quite unpleasant when he tried to speak to him. On seeing a young man, who had been looking at him with excessive interest, begin to head in the direction of the Deputies, Adam gradually melted away behind some nearby trucks. Once out of sight the Marine dissolved into the forest. He became aware of the sound of a breaking branch and crunching leaves off to his left and looking, he noticed the outline of an officer partially obscured by tree trunks. Adam stopped still as the person continued coming closer. As the trees thinned, he saw Deputy T. Lawson striding purposely towards him. Adam had not noticed her at the scene previously.

She gave him a thin-lipped smile as he said cheerily, 'Well hello, 'Tina!''

'Hi ...Mr Wolf!'

'Please! It's Adam!'

Tina stared at him quizzically, before saying softly, 'Adam.'

Tina continued, glancing around furtively as she did so, 'Look Adam ...you must be very careful! Watch out for Taylor!'

'What do you mean?' Adam questioned, surprised by her directness.

Tina looked away and turning back she ran her hand quickly through her fringe letting it bounce back gently, while saying in what was almost a whisper, 'I believe that Taylor has been involved in drug running with local gangs. I ...I am sure that he was involved in the murder of your family and of Paul.'

She glanced away as Adam said incredulously, 'What!'

Adam, sorrowful, thought for a moment and then said almost to himself, 'Even his own nephew!'

Tina looked nervous and turning to leave she cautioned, 'Take care Adam and watch out for him! I'm sorry but I must go. I don't want to be seen talking to you!'

Deputy T. Lawson disappeared back into the trees heading back towards the quarry.

Adam stood aghast, watching until he could see her no more. Then sighing heavily, he turned and, unseen, headed back to his vehicle. He could still hear the loud commotion emanating from the quarry when he arrived at his car. Though by then it was less intense.

He opened the door and sat heavily into the driver's seat. Putting his hand on the window frame he failed to shut the door as he had become so engrossed in his quandary.

The underwater team completed the survey of the quarry floor. As they finished their work waiting ambulances took the three, bloated bodies to the morgue. It did not take long before the weapons in the truck were linked to the horrific murders in Danny's home.

It also didn't take long to officially identify Jeb, Buck and Wade who were well known to the police officers.

Nobody on the force seemed too bothered that the three had died. Some of the law enforcers actually appeared to be quite content!

After sitting in the clearing for over an hour, alone with his thoughts, Adam shut the door and drove away.

Chapter Fourteen
Main Street, Clintburg, Kentucky, USA

Adam had woken early and after taking a refreshing shower he had walked into town stopping for breakfast at Frank's Diner. Frank, who had been a former fire-fighter called the decor retro, but to his customers they felt that it was just plain tired. The waitress refilled Adam's coffee twice before he got up to leave. As he did so he dropped a clutch of dollar bills onto the table to cover the check and the tip. Adam then made his way around the diner asking staff and customers if they had any information that they could give him relating to the deaths of his family. Though most of those that he spoke to were friendly and concerned for his loss, no-body appeared to know anything about the incident and most seemed ill at ease talking about the murders and the fire.

As Adam went to go, Frank came to the door and said

to him, 'Wolf, just a bit of friendly advice. You may be safer to leave this to the police to investigate.'

Adam had known Frank through his youth, as a customer and as someone to pass pleasantries with. The Marine had always felt that he was honest and straight talking.

Adam did wonder why Frank had suggested that he may be 'safer' to leave it to the police. As he pushed the door open Adam looked back at Frank and said bluntly, 'Would you Frank? Would you if it had been your family?'

Frank gave him a half smile and then looked down towards the ground as if he was ashamed of what he had said.

Frank thought for a moment and said, 'Well ...I believe that I would do the same as you. But I would hope that there would be people who liked and admired me enough to warn me of ...potential dangers!'

Adam softened and patted Frank on the upper arm, saying, 'Thanks Frank! I know that you mean well!'

Disappearing through the door Adam next went from store to store along Main Street, questioning anyone he came across. As he went to leave the fourth store his way was blocked by the Sheriff who stood in the open doorway.

'Adam, I've heard that you've been asking questions about our ongoing investigation!'

Adam stared back at him and said nothing.

'I don't want there to be any problems.' The Sheriff stated, before continuing, 'I'm telling you now Adam - you're not to continue making your own enquiries. This is a matter for 'my' Department, and I will update you as soon as I have further information. Do you understand me?'

The last sentence was uttered with great emphasis, and some might have said, an element of menace. But to anyone looking at the scene they would have noticed a man, Adam, who appeared at ease and relaxed, but inside there was an intense fury burning inside him.

He returned the stare of the Sheriff with his own unblinking gaze, and after an excessively long silence, he said coldly, 'I understand you ...Sheriff!'

Carter did not care for the way that the sniper spoke to him. The answer Adam had given could have been interpreted as ambiguous and possibly even disrespectful. Carter noted that Adam did not say that he would desist. However, the Sheriff did not wish to create confrontation - certainly not in public. Adam purposefully walked forward directly towards the Sheriff leaving him no other option, but to step aside as Adam gave him a withering look.

The Sheriff's eyes bored into the back of Adam's head as he departed.

Then as Adam strode down the sidewalk, he heard

Carter sarcastically call after him bitterly, 'Have a nice day, Wolf!'

Listening to the Sheriff's final remarks Adam thought, 'You really 'should not' have said *that,* Carter!'

Chapter Fifteen
Kerri's House, Clintburg, Kentucky, USA

Adam was lying on his bed relaxing. He could not stop running through the sequence of events since he had returned to the town. As he thought, the phone to the side of his bed rang out and at the second ring he answered it.

The youth at the reception said, 'I have a call for you.' And without waiting for an answer, he put it through.

Kerri's mother spoke weakly, 'Hello Adam is that you? It's Madison, Kerri's mother.'

Adam spoke sternly into the phone, 'Hang on Madison. Young man you can either put down your phone now, or I will come to your office and put it down for you.'

His words were intended for the receptionist who he was sure was listening in on the call. There was a gasp and a sudden click on the line as the office clerk's phone abruptly returned to its cradle.

Madison was confused, but Adam continued, 'I'm sorry about that! Madison, is everything okay?'

She blurted out, 'No, it's not Adam, I'm very scared!'

Adam's heart sank as he replied, 'Why?'

'Kerri told me that she was going to collect me this morning and that she would bring Staci. We were all going to go into town to do some shopping. They were meant to be here forty minutes ago. I ...I keep telephoning and she doesn't answer her cell phone or the home phone either. I'm ...I'm so worried Adam.'

Adam asked, 'Have you moved home since I last saw you?'

'Uh ...no ...no ...I haven't ...' she said absent-mindedly before leaving a short pause and then adding dreamily, '...unfortunately!'

Adam said swiftly, 'I'll be there in fifteen minutes to pick you up!' Then added more sympathetically, 'Please don't worry Madison. I will make it all better! I promise you!'

He slowly replaced the handset, a concerned look written harsh across his face. Adam was already dressed needing only to pull his boots on, after which he then grabbed his keys. He ran out of the room slamming the door as he did so before jumping into the car, reversing quickly, and racing out of the parking lot. As he drove past the motel office his angry eyes bored through the windows. Unsurprisingly, the youth was nowhere to be seen.

Coming close to Madison's home Adam saw that she was waiting at her door and on seeing him she ran down the path towards the road, meeting him as his car slewed to a halt. She jumped in and he floored the accelerator rapidly eating up the mile or more of tarmac on the way to Kerri's house.

They slipped down the short driveway through the trees to Kerri's home. It wasn't much of a place he thought to himself. He could tell immediately that something was wrong. Her car was there, and the house was in darkness, whilst the front door lay ominously ajar. Most concerningly, however, halfway down the wooden steps which led from the porch to the potholed mud drive, a child's shoe lay on its side.

Madison broke down in tears as Adam braked hard. Continuing to look at the building, he whispered, 'Wait here!'

He rapidly made his way towards the house and quickly skirting the exterior he cautiously went through the front door. The place was a mess and clearly showed signs of a struggle. However, his heart lifted. He had expected to find Kerri and maybe even Staci's bodies in the interior. The fact that they were not there indicated that the pair may have been taken to use as leverage against Adam.

On the kitchen table Adam found a roughly scrawled note. It said in block capitals at the top, 'DO NOT

TELL THE SHERIFF OR ANYONE ELSE OR WE WILL KILL THEM BOTH.' It then continued, 'Wolf must come alone in a car to the crossroads at Jacksons gas station at 11:00 a.m. tomorrow morning. Do not come armed!'

The note made Adam question his view of what was going on. 'Why would these people ask him 'not' to contact the Sheriff?'

He wondered, '*If* the Sheriff or his Department were in league with them, then maybe the kidnappers did not wish to force the officers into the position of having to make some pretence of acting to foil the criminals? Maybe the very act of informing the Sheriff's Department might somehow force what was going on into the wider world? Or maybe it was just added in because that was what was always said in the movies, and it appeared appropriate? Could it have been a ruse to cover up the involvement of the Law Enforcers? Or maybe there were only some members of the local force who were in on it?'

Adam let his hand, with the note, slowly fall to his side as he considered the possibilities. Unable to come to any firm conclusions he slipped the note into his pocket.

Adam knew the old gas station which had been a fixture for over fifty years. It lay outside of town, not far from the main highway. Declining passing trade had meant that it had been left with no other option but to shut down over ten years before. It had remained increasingly derelict ever since.

Adam went out onto the porch and walked down the steps picking up the little shoe as he did so. He passed it through his hand and gently stroked it as he felt like a deep pit had opened up in his stomach.

Thoughtful, Adam went back to the car and turned to Madison who was in a state of near panic. He tried to say as soothingly as possible, 'They've taken Staci and Kerri to ensure my compliance. I will do everything I can to help them. Do not worry, they will be unharmed! You need to leave town, however, for a few days while I sort this out. Is there anywhere you can go?'

She looked stupefied and broke down in tears again.

'Madison, please! You must help me!'

'Can't we call the police?' She whimpered.

'No, absolutely not!' he said, 'I think it may have something to do with them!'

He thought it telling, that though she continued to cry she slightly nodded her head in agreement.

Eventually she suggested that she could go to stay with her sister who lived with her husband twenty miles away on a farm outside a town called Harrodsville.

They drove back to Madison's home and collected a few things. She quickly called her sister, before they drove off. Adam's anger had been simmering under the surface since he had been informed of the deaths while he was in Afghanistan. However, it had morphed into an uncontrollable rage.

It was all he could do to desperately try to console Madison. He liked her enormously and she had always been kind to him, ever since he was a child. He remembered with great fondness drinking her home-made lemonade on the porch of her house while he chatted happily with Kerri and their other friends on sultry, summer evenings.

They passed much of the journey in silence, broken only by the intermittent whimpering of Madison. He felt sick to his stomach, and he knew that he had brought these horrors on to this innocent, decent family!

As they came closer to Harrodsville, Madison perked up slightly as she began to direct Adam to the farm which lay in a remote spot. Adam wondered if that was a good thing or not, but his options for her were limited and he felt that this was his best one.

Madisons sister, Shirley, ran out of the house at the sound of the vehicle coming down the long track which cut through newly ploughed fields. As Madison climbed out of the car she groaned slightly as her rheumatism began to act up. She fell into her sister's arms in floods of tears while Adam, dropping her luggage, said, 'Thank you for what you are doing. It is very important that nobody knows where Madison is staying. I think you will be safe, but if you get any unusual visitors then you must call your local police immediately.'

Turning to Madison he said, 'You must make sure that you do not contact anyone until this whole mess is sorted out.'

Madison nodded in response, as tears slipped down her face.

Shirley, looked horrified and said, 'What is going on?'

'I can't tell you yet – I am not sure I even know myself!'

He continued, 'Does your husband have a gun?'

Shirley looked even more anxious and replied, 'Well, yes! Two ...two rifles and a shotgun.'

Adam said, 'Ask him to stay home and to keep them loaded! He must not hesitate to use them if he needs to! Madison will fill you in about the recent events.'

Shirley looked absolutely horrified but said, 'Well ... OK ...we will do anything we can to help Madison. I'll call my husband in now from the fields.'

With that Adam returned to the car. As he drove away from the farm, watching the two sisters walking into the farmhouse arm in arm, he felt a great sense of relief. She was safe for the time being and more importantly he could be left to prepare for the next morning.

Unseen, the man with the scar had watched intently from across the road, hidden deep within the woods which bordered the road.

Even further into the trees a Cooper's Hawk rested on the branch of a dead pine tree. He had watched scar face come, and then he watched as the man stealthily made his way back to his vehicle which was hidden in a track half a mile away.

Minutes later the bird burst out in a loud, grating cak-cak-cak call. Then the majestic hawk dropped from its branch into a log slow glide through the trees and onwards into open countryside and towards obscurity.

On the way back to the rendezvous Adam stopped at a small store. He bought some supplies and then he headed to the crossroads to prepare for what was to come.

Far behind scarface continued to track him.

Chapter Sixteen
The outskirts of Clintburg, Kentucky, USA

Adam was driving back via town from Harrodsville when he saw a police car ahead. It was pulled up behind a battered and mud splattered Chevrolet Colorado pickup.

The Chief Deputy Sheriff stood nearby on the grass verge, deep in animated conversation with the man from the Dirty Dollar, Floyd.

Adam eyed them both suspiciously as he drove by. Taylor stared at Adam with a cryptic look on his face whilst Floyd averted his eyes suddenly, as if to hide himself away.

Adam drove on, considering what he had just seen as he tried to fit the awkward pieces into the puzzle. As he did so, Tina's words came back to haunt him.

A strong smell of damp leaves and pine filled the car as he drove on through the forest.

Several miles away on a quiet, dusty road a patrol car slowed to a stop beside a lonely mailbox. It served the local rural community but, on that day, it served a different purpose. The occupant looked around furtively. Then the window slid down and a woman's hand dropped a letter into the box.

Chapter Seventeen
Crossroads at Jacksons gas station,
outside Clintburg, Kentucky, USA

Adam had circled the area around the gas station to familiarise himself with the location. He then drove a short distance down the road before pulling the truck out of sight into a small clearing in the forest. Adam made his way carefully towards the old gas station and scouted out the area ensuring that nobody was lying in wait in the building or even nearby.

Returning to the car he lowered the front side windows so that he could listen for anything out of the ordinary. There was little traffic and through the night he expected to get even less. Adam had turned the car so that he could see the gas station through the windscreen, though the trees partially obscured his view. He ate the sandwich that he had bought at the store and drank a bottle of orange juice. He set his alarm on his watch for

4:00 a.m. Lowering the seat enough so that he could doze while still keeping a clear view of the gas station, he pulled his coat over him and tried to rest. Between the passing cars and the constant thought for the safety of Kerri and Staci he had not slept well. When the alarm went off at four, Adam was half awake.

All was silent apart from the noise of the falling rain which dropped softly, and which had commenced an hour before and showed no sign of stopping.

Adam pulled on his jacket and got out of the car without shutting the door fully. He walked through the trees towards the crossroads keeping out of sight of the highway. Then he sat waiting and watching for forty-five minutes. Hearing nothing Adam returned to the car and drove it the short distance to the gas station forecourt. He looked at his watch as he pulled the key from the ignition.

Adam had parked the car close to the building. He then collected lengths of pipe upturned rubbish bins, empty oil tanks and other detritus that lay about the site. These items were laid in a haphazard way as if they had been there for many years. They had the effect of corralling any vehicle's arrival into a relatively short space close to his car. Adam then combined some old plywood signage rubber piping and two distorted oil drums into a form of cave-like tent. He returned to the car stuffing the rope and knives he had bought in the store, into his trouser pocket before shutting the door. He looked around and seeing nothing of importance slipped into the wood surrounding the gas station and urinated against the trunk of an American plum, though in truth he had no idea of its actual genus. He then listened and carefully surveyed his surroundings before crossing the forecourt and slipping into the hollow under the signage. Any car which arrived would almost certainly pull up between his position and his car. The occupants would naturally be drawn to his vehicle, and he hoped to the building beyond, leaving him in their unguarded rear.

He then lay down and waited. There was a strong smell of gas all around and the concrete forecourt felt uncomfortable after a short time. A truck and two cars drove past in the ensuing hours but after 9:00 a.m. he noted nothing until 10:15 a.m. At that point he heard a vehicle driving fast some distance away, but when it came to the crossroads and the deserted gas station it slowed appreciably. Suddenly, it picked up speed again and drove off. Adam sensed that it was them. They must have felt that they were turning up early to catch him off guard. The newcomers would have seen his car in the forecourt and no doubt were probably surprised. Adam wondered if his plans had gone awry. Could they have parked some distance away and even as he lay there be coming towards the forecourt through the forest from different angles. He prayed that they were both lazy and stupid.

He listened and he waited, just as he had been taught in sniper school. He did his best to control his breathing and his heart rate and then he heard it. Some distance away he detected the sound of the vehicle returning. He recognised the engines roar, but this time it was travelling at a gentler pace. Closing in on the gas station it slowed even more, and as it entered the forecourt it did so at a crawl. The car came to a stop close to where he had expected, and it carried four men in the vehicle. Two in the back with machine guns, whilst the passenger in front had a pistol and the driver held a rifle. The men in the back climbed out, glanced into Adam's empty car, and then walked in unison towards the decaying building. Looking inside they realised that there was no one there and they turned back for instructions shaking their heads as they did so. The passenger pointed them towards the building urging them on, and they started to make their way through the doorless entrance. As they did so the passenger climbed out and stood beside his open door. The driver half-opened his door but remained in his seat.

Adam, who by then held the knives in his hands, slithered out of his makeshift nest then rose to a crouching position as he slowly crept towards the kidnapper's car. All the men intently focused their attention on the gas station. Even so sweat ran down the sides of Adam's temples as he desperately tried to make no noise. As he came close to the passenger some primaeval sense within the man made him half turn towards Adam. He would never turn again. Adam's right-hand darted out and he buried a knife deep into the horrified man's temple. The driver, hearing the thud as the knife hit home and the dying gasp from his conspirator, began to turn. From the corner of his eye, he saw Adam grabbing the pistol from the falling passenger's hand and he tried to swing his rifle towards him. As the driver did so the barrel smashed into the door frame just as a lump of lead bursting from the pistol, smashed through his skull entering just below the nose. Toppling backwards out of his seat his body smashed into the oil spattered floor.

The drivers two colleagues whose total concentration had been focused on the derelict building suddenly turned at the sound of the shot. As they did so Adam caught one in the shoulder and the other kidnapper in the stomach with a round each. The man who had been hit in the gut winced and buckled, but despite his injury he went to raise his machine gun towards Adam to return fire. But as he did so a hail of bullets ripped through his chest and jawbone throwing him lifeless to the floor. The killer who had been hit in the shoulder, falling back, had involuntarily gripped the trigger of his machine gun, and let loose the deadly stream of bullets which had killed his compatriot. Adam raced forward, and as the dead man hit the ground, he managed to kick the machine gun from the other wounded man's grip breaking two of his fingers in the process. He then moved forward and dragged the dead man's body behind the car to hide it from passing traffic.

Adam next returned to the wounded man who was screaming and who was preoccupied with the agony of his upper body wound and his broken fingers. On seeing Adam and the look on the Marine's face his physical pains suddenly became the least of his worries. Adam knelt beside him and said nothing. He just looked into the man's eyes unblinking as his left arm lunged forward, the kitchen knife blade burying deep into the man's hip. The gunman's previous agonies paled into insignificance as Adam slowly twisted the knife.

Yelling out in agony the prostrate man screamed, 'Please ...please. No! No! I didn't want to hurt you. I will tell you anything! Please stop! Pl ...please don't hurt me!'

Adam had always felt that he was compassionate, but as he glared at the man, he was devoid of any compassion. Adam pulled the knife out and then plunged it into the other hip and did the same thing again.

As the man yelled in agony he implored, 'Please! I will tell you anything!'

Tears poured from his eyes as he realised that the man, Adam, who he then looked on with horror and who he had come to kill, was a monster who would probably kill him.

Adam left the knife buried deep in the man's hip whilst his hand remained on the handle saying deliberately, 'You will tell me everything!'

The gunman was dying though he did not know it and he desperately hoped that there may be some chance of survival.

He cried out, 'They have the woman and the child ... they're okay! I swear it! Okay ...but they will kill them whatever you do! They will probably be safe until the others capture you! I ...I can help you! Please ...please don't hurt me!'

Adam's withering eyes stared through the man who lay before him saying, as he questioned, 'Where are they?'

'They're in the old Barker place. It's ...' he winced as a spasm of pain ran through him before continuing, '... about five miles out of town on the east route.'

Adam knew the place. Knowing that the man had little time left he asked, 'How many of them are there?'

The blood loss was taking its toll on the dying man, and he was beginning to slip slowly in and out of consciousness. He had defecated involuntarily, and the stench was overpowering. He whimpered, 'There are ... um ...maybe, uh ...twenty or more of them and they ...' His words trailed off into gibberish.

Adam shook him and the man continued, '...they have many automatic weapons ...please, help me ...please ...'

'Are member of the sheriff's Department helping them?' Adam asked.

'Police ... Yes, the police ... Poli ...'

At that point the individual began to shiver and lost all lucidity. Adam noted that he was cold to the touch.

Adam pulled the knife out of the man who hardly seemed to notice though his rate of decline increased, as did his blood loss.

Adam walked over to the driver and pushed him back into the rear of their own car followed by the other dead gunman and his dying friend. He then leant over the last man who lay in a heap on the floor and manhandled him back into the front passenger seat. Adam had searched each of the bodies for weapons and ammunition and had thrown them on to the concrete forecourt.

The car was still running, and Adam climbed in and drove the vehicle back to where he had been parked among the trees during the night. He drove the car deep into the scrub until it would move forward, no more, before turning the engine off.

As Adam climbed out over the undergrowth and unknown to him, the dying man who had been stuffed unceremoniously into the back of the car gasped his last. The thug would never again assault his ex-wife or his children or anyone else for that matter. Adam jogged back to his own vehicle and picked up the rifle, machine guns and a couple of loose clips that lay scattered around before throwing them into the rear of his car. He looked across the concrete floor which was covered in blood, and he breathed in deeply before letting out a determined sigh. Turning the engine on, Adam slowly pulled out onto the highway and headed towards the Barker place with a sense of finality hanging over him. He ran the window down to let in a blast of air to clear his lungs of the stench of oil, faeces, and death.

The man with the scar above his eye had lain in wait, just as Adam had, through the night, hidden among the trees. He had been watching the unfolding events and had left his hiding place near the gas station ten minutes before Adam had left the forecourt. He had run through the trees and scrub, the quarter mile to where his car had been hidden the day before, some way down a side road. He was supremely fit, and he covered the distance easily.

By the time he was back in his vehicle he was in time to see Adam through the trees hiding the kidnapper's car. When Adam drove off in his own vehicle, the man waited a few minutes before slowly pulling out onto the highway, following Adam's route. He instinctively looked in his rear-view mirror and then ran the windows down letting the car fill with fresh air. The man had a very determined look and keeping one hand on the wheel he rhythmically stroked the vivid scar across his face.

The radio station he had on in the background began to play Rod Stewart's, 'The first cut is the deepest.' Scar-face suddenly burst into a wide grin which showcased his broken teeth and a single gold incisor.

Chapter Eighteen
Sheriff's Department, Clintburg,
Kentucky, USA

Deputy Chief Jervis Taylor had started early each day. He had done so every day since the death of his nephew, Paul. The stars still sparkled in the sky each time he arrived at work. He was surrounded by piles of old, case files which were strewn across his desk. Jervis had taken them out of storage, and he was slowly and methodically ploughing through them in an effort to find something ...anything.

He was very tired, and he felt his eyes glazing over at times. Taking a sip of cold coffee from the mug which lay on his desk, he continued on. The door of his office was slightly ajar and just after 9:20 a.m. one of the junior officers came to him and said in a slightly embarrassed tone, 'Deputy Chief, something has just been delivered in the post. I think you should see it.'

The Deputy Chief thought the man's demeanour was a touch strange. He had also stayed at the door giving the impression that he had to come with the officer. Jervis got up and went out to the officer's desk and noted that only half of the post was opened, and it had been placed in a neat pile on the right. The plastic bin that sat beside the officer's chair was full of torn envelopes and one empty coke can. The young man pointed at the only open letter in the centre of the desk, with the torn envelope which it had come in, lying beside it.

Taylor went to pick the sheet up and the young officer said, 'Sir, it may be best not to touch that, there may be fingerprints on it.'

Jervis's interest was piqued as he glanced at the officer appreciatively.

He looked at the document and immediately recognised the note. It was exactly the same as the one that he had found in Paul's hand after he had 'apparently' committed suicide. Like the other, this note was also typed. Somebody was clearly unhappy that he had withheld that confession which implicated his nephew. So, they were leaving nothing to chance by sending a second note to the station. 'Fingerprint this immediately he snapped to the young officer!'

'Yes sir.'

The officer picked the sheet up with a set of tweezers before putting it in a plastic bag which he had already collected, on the way to see Taylor. The Deputy Chief who was heading back to his room turned back and smiled, 'You've done well, thank you.'

Half an hour later the young officer returned and said, 'There is only one set of prints on the letter and two sets of prints on the envelope. The prints on the letter are mine. As far as the envelope goes one set of prints are mine and the other belonged to the postman.'

'How could you be certain that it was the postman's prints?' Jervis said.

'I checked several of the other envelopes we received today and several that we received yesterday. I had to go through the rubbish bag outside for that.'

'That's good police work!' Jervis said.

'Thank you, Sir!' He chirped as he left the room.

This letter could not be hidden from the investigation now. That was clearly the intention of whoever sent it.

Jervis had a very determined look on his face, and he was angry – very angry indeed. He was left with two certain conclusions. Firstly, Paul was murdered. Secondly, he was murdered to give him up as a patsy for the killings at Danny's home.

He stared out of the window in contemplation looking across the roof tops into the distance. His concentration was broken by the same junior officer from before.

'Sir, there was another letter in the mail, and it is addressed to you. I didn't open it as it is marked, personal.'

He handed it to Taylor before turning and leaving the room. The Deputy Chief waited for the door to shut before he opened it. As he read the contents his mood darkened, and his expression intensified. His powerful hand clenched into a fist crushing the letter into a ball which he then slipped into his pocket. Jervis then left for the day, without saying anything to anyone.

Chapter Nineteen
The old Barker place, outskirts of Clintburg, Kentucky, USA

A battered, old, black Buick made its way out of Clintburg. The route that the driver had taken was quite peculiar. Exiting the town to the west the man had taken a very long and circuitous route around Clintburg to eventually get to the eastern side.

Soon after leaving Clintburg the car had slid into a track and come to a halt behind a derelict wooden barn. Enough of the building remained to disguise the presence of the vehicle to passing traffic. On exiting the vehicle, the driver had taken his time to survey the area to ensure that he was completely alone. He then took some tools and a package from the trunk and proceeded to change the number plate, putting the original back in the trunk along with the tools. Opening a holdall stuffed with clothing which sat on the backseat of the car he changed his outfit, putting the garb that he had left home in back in the bag. Shutting the trunk, he looked back towards the road through the broken boards of the barn. Then he went on his way.

The driver was unrecognizable from the man who had turned down the track to the barn. He had changed into boots, faded jeans and a red check shirt. The man was also wearing an overly large pair of cheap sunglasses which would have better suited a woman. The filthy nylon baseball cap that he wore had its peak pulled excessively low over the man's face giving him a rather comic look for anyone who had caught sight of him. The day was overcast and the need for the sunglasses seemed at odds with the weather. Also incongruous was the fact that both sun visors had been pulled down towards the windscreen, slightly shading the interior of the car.

Comfortably slicing around a shallow bend in the road, the driver noticed an oncoming car a hundred yards ahead and approaching fast. Taking one of his hands from the steering wheel he propped his elbow against the door and placed the palm of his hand on the side of his face further obscuring it. Once the vehicle had gone past, he glanced in the rear-view mirror and put his hand back on the steering wheel.

As he followed the path towards his destination the same repeating pattern occurred whenever an oncoming car was encountered.

Finally, he noted ahead of him the road climbing up through a forested area. The man glanced in his rear mirror and seeing no other traffic and no oncoming vehicles either, he began to accelerate. The driver knew the area very well and he also knew what he was looking for. Coming close to the brow of the hill he lowered his window to listen for anything unusual. Looking in his mirrors and ahead of him once more, on seeing that the coast was clear he swerved the car violently without indicating. The man headed into a barely visible track that was partially overgrown and which led deep into the forest. He drove excessively fast, and the car bounced violently as did he. However, the driver was very competent and had a determined look on his face which showed that he would not be swayed. Coming to a small clearing he spun the car around and turned the engine off even before the wheels had come to a stop. Then he sat without moving listening through the open window. He heard nothing but the wind in the trees and some noises from the vehicle as it creaked and groaned while it cooled down. The man then waited a further ten minutes, waiting for the forest bird's calls return to normal, signalling that all was as it should be. Once satisfied he slowly opened the door and grabbed a camouflage jacket from the passenger seat, before pulling it on.

Looking around he popped the trunk and grabbed a

long object which was sheathed in a blanket. He took the makeshift cover off and threw it back into the trunk before shutting it. The driver then walked purposefully into the forest, the high-powered sniper rifle in his hand.

As the trees began dropping away from him into the valley below, he took his time looking for a spot where the growth was denser and yet he still had a good view of the Barker place in the valley floor and the road which led to it, far below.

Finding a perfect site, he lay down and set up his weapon letting it rest on its bipod. It was a military grade M24 SWS sniper rifle. They were not available to the public and he had come by it when he had found it in the back of an abandoned car. It may have been used by drug dealers who had themselves been dealt their final blow. Liking the M24 and wondering if one day it may come in useful, he had kept it.

The man lay down behind the rifle and looking through the scope he scanned the whole area. He noticed two cars in front of the main building and occasionally he would see various men walking around the area, gun in hand, as if they were on guard duty. The individuals didn't complete the task very well and seemed to see it as a chore.

He sat down against a nearby American beech tree partially obscured by distance and the forest. Then he settled in for a long wait. As he did so, he became more aware of the repetitive hammering sound of a nearby Red-headed Woodpecker. The haunting echo of it was strangely comforting.

Chapter Twenty
Fry Hollow, near the Barker place,
outskirts of Clintburg, Kentucky, USA

Adam had his boot to the floor. As he drove, he reached over into the passenger footwell and picked up an oil stained, baseball cap which he pulled low over his face.

He saw a few cars on the road and a couple of tractors going about their business. Nothing to cause him concern. His mind wandered as he thought about Kerri and Staci and what he would face ahead of him.

The journey was uneventful and as he came to a forested region the road started to climb and his vehicle began to labour. The engine eased as he reached the brow of the hill and commenced the descent towards the old Barker place which lay deep in the valley. He did not notice the small, overgrown track off to one side which cut into the forest. Nor did he see the fresh tyre tracks which led on to the man and the battered, old, black

Buick which lay disguised among the trees. The other man with the scar who passed by the same spot shortly afterwards did not notice anything either.

His sole focus was on Adam.

As the valley floor loomed ahead Wolf pulled the cap a little lower and pressed himself deeper into the seat. Off to one side he saw a large, dirt track which had clearly seen a great deal of traffic. It cut straight into the forest for approximately one hundred yards and then turned off at a sharp angle which meant that the property was impossible to see. Adam surreptitiously glanced at the area to check if there were any people visible. Seeing nothing he drove on at the same speed and began to climb the road on the far side of the valley. He did consider that if sentries had been posted that they may well be hidden. Adam crested the brow of the hill and continued for half a mile before gently slowing down and turning off into a clearing in a place called Fry Hollow. He parked the car behind a large rock outcrop.

Adam had not wanted to stop before just in case somebody was listening to the sound of his vehicle. He climbed out of the car and unloaded the weapons from the trunk. The only sounds to be heard were those of the forest, rustling leaves, and songbirds. Sounds which had always given him great comfort ever since his youth. Adam checked all the weapons and made sure that they were all fully loaded and then stuffed his pockets full of ammunition. He also took two M67 fragmentation grenades. Adam had been surprised to see them on the back seat of the vehicle that had arrived at the Jacksons gas station with the kidnappers on board. They had clearly been prepared for anything in their encounter with Adam.

Wolf turned towards the forest and began the trek back up to the brow of the hill. Soon after setting off, he suddenly stopped. Adam had heard a vehicle passing by, following the same route as he had taken. The car was not travelling very fast but had been maintaining its speed. He watched through the trees as it passed by catching occasional glimpses of it through the gaps in the swathe of tree trunks. He was relieved to see that the car drove on until it could be heard no more. Adam turned and headed to the top of the hill. Wolf was correct. The car had continued on in much the same way as Adam had. The other driver also did not want to give away his intensions.

The man with the scar had just caught sight of Adam's car disappearing behind rocks just as he had come to the brow of the hill. When he was far enough away, he too turned off into the forest, parking his vehicle deep enough in that it was not visible. He quickly jumped out and grabbed a rifle and a pistol from the trunk. He then took a Matthews Atlas bow and a quiver full of Easton Full Metal Jacket arrows with Iron Will

SB125 Broadhead arrow points which he slipped over his shoulder. He enjoyed working with a bow above all other weapons and its near silent use suited him, particularly in his current hunt.

The stocky, scar faced, man began to jog slowly through the forest doing his best to minimise the noise whilst making up the time to catch up with his quarry. He knew that he was under pressure now and that the game was afoot.

On reaching the brow of the hill he came to a halt and crouched down behind the trunk of a magnificent Tulip Poplar which had a pronounced lean caused by the prevailing winds. He enjoyed the feel of the roughness of the bark. Being alone in nature, against the elements always had a profoundly positive and cathartic effect on him. He knew not why! The bowman looked down into the valley and saw the Barker place standing in a clearing with a couple of small outbuildings beside. Nearby he noted two vehicles untidily parked. He also noticed armed men walking about the site. They did not appear to be professional, and he did not get the impression that they had had military training. However, he suspected that there could still have been others who were of a much higher calibre and who chose to lurk in the shadows.

Far down the slope scar face had come to a stop. He watched Adam very closely. Very closely indeed!

He slipped his hand into the quiver and pulled out an arrow. Slipping it into position he drew back the string and took aim.

He had killed before and he was preparing to kill again!

Chapter Twenty-one
American hazelnut thicket, near the Barker place, outskirts of Clintburg, Kentucky, USA

Adam had been making his way cautiously down the slope when it happened.

He heard an almost imperceptible crack, as a twig broke near to him. Wolf turned suddenly, but he was too late. One of the gang members was clearly a very skilled and cunning hunter. The thug had been hidden amidst a thicket of American hazelnut and wild grasses. He was dressed in a military-grade, sniper ghillie suit. The man was totally undetectable unless he moved. And he only moved when Adam was close and when the Marine had his back to him.

Adam looked into the eyes of the would be killer and saw the machete in his hand descending at great speed directly at Wolf's temple. It was clear from the face of this gang member that he liked to kill and that he also enjoyed inflicting pain. It all happened so fast that Adam could hardly take it in! The angry, satisfied eyes of the hunter suddenly changed. Adam saw the instant, total shock within them as the tungsten arrowhead drove deep into the back of the skull, through the cerebellum and beyond. The arm with the machete which was so forcefully hunting its target suddenly fell to the right as did the rest of the man's body. He was dead before he hit the ground.

Wolf instantly dropped to a crouch, looking for the source of the arrow. Then, stunned, he saw scar face with a second arrow already in position. Suddenly, the archer let it lose and it came relentlessly at full pelt in Adam's direction. He had no time to move, which saved his life. The arrow passed his upper body missing by inches. But the tungsten did find its intended target. A second gang member, again in a ghillie suit, had come from his own hiding place and was about to shoot Adam with his Glock 17. The arrow drove straight through the man's upper chest causing catastrophic damage. It was not a clean kill. It was, however, a kill. Adam looked back at the dying man as he desperately tried, in a futile attempt, to cling to life. Lacking any understanding, Adam turned back towards the archer. Then Wolf stood up tall and looked, relieved, at the cruelly disfigured face, the face of his friend, Chief. John Riggs was smiling, and he gave Adam a slow wave as he ushered him onwards.

Adam had never felt happier to see that brave Cherokee, than he did at that point. Riggs slipped another arrow into place in readiness for what was to come.

Adam waved back and then leant down, prising the machete from the hand of the dead man. Then Wolf recommenced his trek deeper into the valley. He was angry with himself at having been caught in such a trap. He knew that, but for Riggs, he would be dead. His fear for Kerri and Staci had made him reckless. He knew that he could not make another mistake, as if he did their fate and his might well be sealed.

Throughout, the incident was watched through the scope of an M24 SWS sniper rifle. Beside an American beech tree, the man from Clintburg, who had arrived in the battered Buick, briefly took his eye away from the scope. As he did, he tried to understand what was truly going on.

Then he stopped wondering as he saw movement off to his left. He did not shift his body, instead he only moved his eyes. He was certain, there was 'something' there and it was moving slowly in the bush. Then the bushes stopped making their unnatural movement. He slid his rifle to the side and slowly repositioned himself. Watching through the scope he breathed in deep and cupped the trigger with his finger. Then the head of a black bear popped up, looking about at some unseen distraction. Its nose twitched as it carefully smelt the air for anything untoward. Contenting itself, the curious head disappeared again and went back to the huckleberry bushes as it fed on their nutritious fruit.

Relieved, the sniper turned back to the task at hand.

Chapter Twenty-two
The Barker place, outskirts of Clintburg, Kentucky, USA

Adam proceeded with greater caution as he realized that the gang members were not all the untrained hicks that he had initially taken them for. His path was followed at a distance by Chief who gave him cover. The use of the silent arrows meant that their presence had not been announced.

Chief saw Adam crouch down and signal to him to take out one of the two guards who were visible to them. Chief lent against the trunk of a magnificent black cherry tree. Then reducing his breathing and steadying his aim he tracked one of the guards as he turned first one corner and then a second of the largest building on the site. Once out of sight of the other guard and before the gang member passed in front of a window Chief let loose his arrow. It cut deep into the man's back, slicing through his left kidney and grazing his spine. The guard fell to his knees and dropped his rifle letting his hands go to his chest looking for whatever had caused him such intense pain. The arrowhead was buried deep in his torso and had not penetrated his front. A low gurgling moan emanated from him, which though not loud was just audible to the other guard. Suddenly the injured man saw what had caused his predicament as a second arrow pierced his chest rupturing his heart as it went, before poking through the chest wall and then through his right hand. He fell forward with a thud as the life swiftly ebbed from him.

The second guard made his way to the back of the building, rifle at the ready. He called out as he went, 'Carson, are you O.K.?'

The closer he got to the rear of the structure the more nervous he got, especially as Carson did not reply. The next arrow drove through the side of the second guard's chest, breaking ribs and piercing one lung. He fell to the side in shock and in agony. As he did so the round in his rifle fired as his trigger finger tensed in pain. The bullet drove harmlessly into the ground. The second arrow which cut his carotid artery in his neck meant that he bled out quickly, though the presence of Adam and Chief had been announced to all.

Suddenly, a shot from high in the valley rang out and the Marines saw a sniper in a ghillie outfit fall from behind the trunk of an Eastern White Pine tree where he had hidden. Unknown to the Chief and Adam, the rifleman had broken cover from a thicket he had been hiding in when he heard the second guard call out. On finding his target he had taken aim directly at Adam's heart. The would-be killer had taken his time as he felt that he was unseen. That delay was enough to allow the man from Clintburg high in the valley to lock on with his scope. He breathed out and slowly put pressure on the trigger. The shot from the M24 SWS sniper rifle was lethal as it burst through teeth and gum before bursting out through the back of the other sniper's head. Satisfied, the man from Clintburg reloaded and nestled back into the trunk of the American Beech. Just as he did so a faint breeze brushed his face bringing with it the faint, fragrant scent of a nearby Sassafras tree.

Adam and Chief looked at each other questioningly. Chief shrugged as if to say, 'I don't know who that is!'

Before they could consider matters any further, the front door of the building burst open and a succession of men carrying an assortment of weapons spewed out. Others still, opened windows and poked their weapons through. Though they remained in the shadows, the sight of the muzzles of their weapons was enough to give away their positions and the man from Clintburg began to pick them off, one by one. The M24 SWS sniper rifle was immensely powerful, and the rounds easily punctured the wooden walls before slicing through the gunmen. Adam switched from the machete and began firing his machine gun. Chief swapped to a rifle as he began to shoot the running men. The gang members had burst out with gusto, but as they saw their comrades begin to fall around them, they headed for cover. They soon found that they were pinned down and given the positions of Adam, Chief and the unknown sniper above they made for easy pickings.

Suddenly, Adam saw the Sheriff and Floyd burst from the door heading toward one of the outbuildings. The two running men made for difficult targets, but the man from Clintburg managed to hit the Sheriff in the thigh with a bullet which had been aimed at Floyd. It was enough to slow the officers progress, though Floyd did not offer the injured Sheriff any help. Reaching the door Floyd was desperately fumbling with the padlock to open it. Adam had seen their flight and he had circled the building to come up on their rear.

As Floyd struggled with the lock, a bullet splintered the door beside him making him jump in fright. Turning he saw the Sheriff pointing his gun at his chest and shouting for Floyd to help him. Floyd didn't know what scared him more, but he did believe that the Sheriff would kill him if he refused him assistance. He ran like a scared chicken into the open space and grabbed the Sheriff before dragging him behind the building which he had tried fruitlessly to unlock. Then the two changed their initial plan and deserted the outbuilding making their way off into the forest in an attempt to escape. Neither one of them cared what fate was to befall their comrades. The sound of gunfire filled the valley, though it was gradually beginning to diminish. The two of them were one hundred yards deeper into the forest and looking back they felt some sense of relief. The Sheriff was in agony, gripping his leg wound with one hand while his other arm, gun in hand, hung around Floyd for support.

Floyd stuttered out, 'Sheriff, I ...I will be much faster on my ...own. Let me run ahead and I will get help and then I can ...come back for you!'

Carter stared at Floyd in complete disgust as he responded with an animalistic snarl, 'You are going nowhere without me! If you try to then you will end up coughing out lead!'

Floyd felt like breaking down in tears as he said, 'No ... no, of ...course I will help you. You can trust ...me! Honest!'

Carter had always despised Floyd, but never more so than at that point.

The Sheriff looked back at the carnage below and then turned to Floyd and said, 'Come on let's get going, I need to get to a hospital, fast!'

They took two paces forward and suddenly stopped dead. Stepping out from behind the trunk of a Sweet-gum tree, Adam stood, machete in hand, blocking their path. The look on the Marine's face was enough to send a chill down the spines of both men. Floyd was transfixed with fear, but the Sheriff twisted his hand to get a shot at Adam with his handgun. As the recognition of their predicament had first dawned on them, Adam had already begun raising his arm up high. The machete stood tall above him and before the Sheriff could take aim it fell at tremendous speed slicing through the Sheriffs knuckles and continuing on, deep into Floyd's chest cavity, opening up a gaping hole. Floyd looked down at the wound just as he fainted and fell to the floor taking the officer with him. He made no sound as he slowly died. The Sheriff, brave though he was, who had a grandstand view of events began to whimper as he lay next to Floyd with an intimate view of his blood-soaked lung. The agony of the officer's leg and knuckles was nothing to the well-founded fear that he had begun to feel. He knew that he was defenceless since the gun had fallen from his useless fingers.

He turned to Adam and looked into the face of death as he did so.

He begged, 'N ...n ...no ...please ...Wolf! I ...had come to arrest Fl ...Floyd. He killed your brother ...ple ... please...'

Adam looked down at him and said, 'It's too late for your lies!'

He took the Sheriff's own handcuffs and locked his hands behind his back and around the trunk of a young, White Ash tree. He then tore strips from the Sheriffs uniform shirt and roughly bound his wounds.

Satisfied, Adam slipped down the slope and back to the valley floor. Between the crossfire from Chief and the unknown man from Clintburg few of the kidnappers were still alive.

Adam made his way to the outbuilding to see what Floyd and the Sheriff had been heading towards. He slammed the machete into the padlock and at the second hit, it flew off. Opening the door, he found Kerri and her daughter Staci. They were tied to a chain which hung from one of the wooden supports. They were both petrified, understandably. Adam knelt beside them and stroking Staci's face to calm her, he sliced through their bonds.

Adam whispered, 'You're safe now! Follow me and keep quiet!'

Neither said a word but just crept out of the door behind him.

He then ushered them to the rear of the building and said, 'Go up into the forest after fifty feet or so you will see a large boulder. Shelter there and I will come for you soon.'

Kerri cried out in desperation, 'Please, Adam, don't leave us!'

'Don't worry, I will return soon!' he responded encouragingly.

Watching them go, he then turned and took the grenades from his pockets. Creeping close to the building he lobbed, first one and then the other through the windows of the main building. He ran back taking cover behind the outbuilding just in time to hear the blasts. He doubted that anything inside would have survived that, and he was right.

The remaining men were shocked to see the building destroyed and they tried to make a run for it. But all they served to do was to make themselves easier targets.

The firefight had been brutal. The few kidnappers who survived did not last long, dying from their wounds before the emergency services arrived.

Adam searched the building and found large quantities of drugs and piles of used bills. There were also many dead bodies. He picked up four large sports bags which he found lying about and filled them with cash and three plastic packs of drugs and then he departed.

Before the first Sheriff's Department vehicles arrived Chief, Adam, Kerri, and her daughter Staci had long left the scene along with the Sheriff who had been unceremoniously stuffed into the trunk of Adam's car. Adam gave one of the sports bags to Chief to take with him. They were watched through the sniper scope by the man from Clintburg who remained, surveying the scene.

Chapter Twenty-three
Hickory tree above the Barker place,
outskirts of Clintburg, Kentucky, USA

On the crest of a heavily forested ridge, which over-looked the area, a majestic Hickory tree stood alone among a swathe of American Basswood, Sourwood, Red Maple and White Oak. Though it stood alone – it was not lonely. Crouched behind its great trunk a uniformed woman studied the valley below through binoculars. The carnage was obscene. Having drunk her fill of the slaughter she let the binoculars fall to her side, held by the strap which lay across her chest. Her face, initially shocked, broke into a grotesque, cruel, Iagoesque smile. Her own very personal vendetta had been set in motion. Savouring the intensity of her feelings for a few moments, she rose and picked her way back through the trees towards her car.

Chapter Twenty-four
The Barker place, outskirts of Clintburg, Kentucky, USA

The forest had been alive with birdsong until the fire-fight started. The gunfire had drowned out the sweet sounds of nature and quickly frightened the creatures away. But as the valley drifted back to its more natural state the birds began to return. Far off in the forest the sound of a young, male Wild Turkey could be heard echoing along the valley floor. The distinctive gobble call was being directed at prospective females. Then came the hammering of the industrious Red-headed woodpecker. It had returned to its work enlarging a cavity in a tree close to where the man from Clintburg lay. He found the sound quite cathartic. Shortly afterwards the other birds returned, foremost among them, the Blue Jay. It's loud, squeaky mechanical sound reminded him of his childhood. There was, however, no sign of the black bear who had disappeared along with the fruit from the huckleberry bush.

The man from Clintburg had been about to pack up and leave, but he had decided to wait a while longer. That was fortuitous. The sniper who lay beside the American Beech had been scanning the valley for movement when he saw the sudden glint of sunlight on a pair of binoculars which peaked out from behind a Hickory tree on the other side of the valley.

'Who are you?' he thought to himself.

Then he saw the binoculars drop, revealing the woman's face. He knew instantly who she was. The gradually expanding smile of satisfaction and evil written bold across her face told him why she was there.

Unseen, he watched her as she disappeared. He knew that the intense level of gunfire and explosions would have concerned the local farmers and one or more of them would have contacted the Sheriff's department.

The man from Clintburg made his way back to his car and headed off before the emergency services arrived. He retraced his original route and changed his appearance back to what it had been. Then he swapped the number plates again before re-entering Clintburg unseen and unnoticed.

Chapter Twenty-five
The Sheriff's home, outskirts of Clintburg, Kentucky, USA

Chief had made his own way, driving back to his mother's place and another healthy meal.

Adam had gone straight to Kerri's home dropping her and her daughter off. He then headed away with the unhappy Sheriff. After a mile he pulled into a clearing in some woods near the road. Opening the trunk, he questioned the Sheriff as to where he lived, then he shut the trunk again and drove to the property. Adam wondered why Carter had been so forthcoming and he couldn't help but consider if it was a trap. However, the Sheriff's spirits had lifted once Adam had bound his wounds in the forest and he felt that he had what he desperately needed - a chance.

Adam continued on before turning off into a forest track just beyond a large rock outcrop which forced a bend in the road. Shortly after he did so he crossed a small wooden bridge which stretched over a meandering river. Looking along the watercourse itself, he saw a substantial Beaver lodge a hundred yards upstream. He noticed that the water was alive with industrious Beavers as he headed onwards into the trees.

The Sheriff's home was little short of palatial, and it sat alone amidst a great clearing in a forest of pine. The scent from the trees was intoxicating and powerful. Adam dragged the weeping Sheriff from the trunk and up the steps into the house. Once there he handcuffed him to the stair bannisters. Then he returned to the car and grabbed the drugs and one bag of money. He hid the drugs and some of the money in various locations inside the house and in the separate double garage which stood ten feet from the main building. Adam then put the remaining money in the open bag on top of the kitchen table. Returning to the garage he grabbed a can of fuel which was probably used for the ride on mower which stood nearby.

Heading back to the house he found some matches in the kitchen and then proceeded to soak the living room with fuel. The Sheriff looked on in horror as he frantically begged for mercy.

Adam turned to him and said softly, 'What mercy did my family or anyone else receive?'

Then he lit a magazine that he found on a side table

and tossed it into the living room. There was a loud whomp sound as the room caught alight. He felt the sudden flash of heat across his exposed skin. The Sheriff had given up begging and was desperately trying to pull himself free. Adam looked at him before turning to leave.

As the car pulled away from the house, he could see the structure well alight with clouds of smoke billowing from its roof and open windows. The air was filled with the stench of the burning wood and man-made materials. He could also hear the fruitless screams of the Sheriff.

He ran down the car windows to let in a constant stream of fresh, cool air. Driving on to the highway, he took no pleasure in what he had done, but he did feel a great sense of justice being served – his type of justice!

Chapter Twenty-six
Windy Pines Motel, Clintburg, Kentucky, USA

Adam lay on the bed fast asleep. Unusually for him he had not woken early and had slept on through until 11:00 a.m. He may well have slept longer but for the cheap paper-thin curtains which he had pulled over the large glass window which fronted the room. The glaring sunlight flickered across his eyelids and almost imperceptibly he felt the warmth of the sun on his skin. His eyes opened slowly, and he moved gently on the bed stretching as he did so. Adan let his head roll to the side, and he looked at the ill-fitting curtain. It covered 'most' of the glass but none of the frame which meant that it had a squared off halo of light bursting through on each side.

The phone rang and the receptionist said, 'I have a call for you.'

'Put it through ...and then put the phone down. You

probably have a very good idea of what will happen if you do not!' Adam said ominously.

The call was put through and without word the receptionists phone clicked off instantly.

'Adam was surprised by the identity of the caller, but not what he had to say.'

It was a short call and when it had finished Adam replaced the handset thoughtfully.

He took a deep breath, held it, and then slowly exhaled as he thought to himself, 'It's a new day!'

He lay there feeling a sense of relief. A sense of completion. Hard as it was, he could move on once more with his life, though it would never be the same again.

Twenty minutes later he gradually roused himself and took a long refreshing shower. Getting dressed, he noticed the billowing steam which had moved from the bathroom into the bedroom. He looked up at the extractor fan which didn't work. Nothing seemed to work very well in the motel, even the receptionist.

The noise of Tina's vehicle and the crunching of the loose gravel had announced her arrival to the desk clerk who had been dozing in his chair in the reception room. A half smoked joint lay on the floor beside him where it had fallen over an hour before leaving it's tell-tale sweet, smoky smell hanging heavy in the air. Fortunately, the stench of the weed masked his own foul, very personal, unwashed stench. The youth wiped the sleep from his eyes as he crept over to the window to get a better view. He watched as Tina purposefully walked over to Adam's door.

The receptionist then made several running commentary call's to Sheriff Carter's phone, though he was only able to leave answerphone messages. He was not reporting a crime, rather he was assisting a crime to be committed and more importantly to be recorded.

After getting dressed Adam packed his bag. As he finished, he turned on hearing a knock at the door. He was glad of the interruption as the musty smell of the room was beginning to get to him. It crossed his mind that he had heard a car pull up nearby and oddly enough not outside the room. It had not been long before and he had paid it little attention.

Adam opened the door and saw Tina standing before him. He took a welcome lungful of fresh air as he looked at her. Adam gave her the warmest smile he could muster, before looking her up and down and saying, 'Ahhh, 'Deputy' T. Lawson! How lovely to see you! Please come in.'

As he said the words while standing just inside the door his head turned into the room and his palm came up, both actions forming an invitation to enter.

As she slipped her weapon from its holster, she was bemused by the emphasis he had put on her title, 'Deputy'. But she passed over it as she would kill Wolf regardless. Then suddenly his head and body whipped back, lightning fast, and his hand rose, before chopping down on her gun arm in a violent parry. When he had looked at her Adam had noticed the clip on her holster had been released, ready for a quick draw. He knew what was coming – he had been warned. Tina was utterly stunned as she saw his other hand driving directly at her face in a clenched fist. But it would never connect. At that moment her whole body lunged to the left and she fell to the floor as the gun fell from her hand skittering loudly across the tarmac.

Adam looked down at her prone body and the small hole through the side of her uniform shirt - the trickle of blood oozing from her chest and colouring the material a deep crimson. She looked up at Adam disbelieving. As she did so, Chief Deputy Sheriff Taylor emerged from behind a parked car and came into her vision as he re-holstered his weapon.

'How …How, did you know?' she spluttered as blood began to fill her lungs.

Adam looked down at the pathetic sight and said, 'It was clear to me that you truly 'had' lost someone that you loved deeply. However, when you suggested that it was Paul, something just didn't feel right. I knew that Paul had loved his uncle like a father, and it was a real stretch to accept that this would not have been reciprocated. Also, Paul may have kept your supposed relationship from people here, but not from me.'

Jervis stared at her in utter disgust as Adam continued, 'Who, really, was it you lost?'

Her head turned away from them both as she slowly pushed herself over onto her back and looked up at the sky at the gently passing clouds as a cool breeze brushed her cheeks. Tears began to slide down the sides of her face as she said tenderly, 'Wade ...It was Wade! I loved him soooo much!'

She sighed heavily as she coughed up blood, 'He died because of 'your' family and his supposed buddies. Why didn't your brother just keep out of it all! ...I wanted you all to pay!'

'No wonder you had to keep 'that' relationship quiet in your post! He was hardly a respectable pillar of the community!'

She turned and sneered at Adam as she whispered, 'You didn't know him like I knew him. He was ...a wonderful guy ...'

Her words had trailed off as she finished and Taylor said bitterly, 'He was a low life just like you!'

But she heard none of it, as the life had already ebbed from her.

Adam looked around and could see nobody except the disappearing face of the youth in the reception. On seeing Adam glance in his direction, he had ducked behind his counter. Adam thought that maybe the residents had been too scared to look out at the commotion or more likely, there were no residents.

Jervis followed Adam's eyes and seeing the reception

he said, 'I will be paying that young man a visit soon. Jaxon is going to go on a very long holiday at the expense of the State.'

Adam turned to Jervis and put out his hand and as they shook, he said, referring to the morning telephone call, 'Thanks for tipping me off earlier, though I had kind of expected as much from 'Deputy' T. Lawson. How did you know?'

'I had suspected Lawson for some time. I regret that I had not acted before, but it was difficult – I just didn't know who I could trust! Once Paul ...was ...was murdered, I began to put the pieces together and to watch her more closely. It was clear to me that Paul was being framed. After coming to that conclusion, it was a small step towards the understanding - that so were you!'

Opening the door wider the Sheriff stood nonchalantly before him - or at least the former Chief Deputy who had become the Sheriff overnight. 'Congratulations on your promotion Sheriff!' Adam quipped.

'Thank you! Adam it's come as a bit of a surprise and in some ways, it is down to you.'

Adam smiled and replied, 'Please come in. I'm afraid I can't offer you anything as the minibar seems to have been removed some time ago.'

The Sheriff walked in and announced to Adam, 'I just felt that I should talk to you before you left.'

Adam said nothing and waited for the Sheriff to

speak again. 'It's clear now that the Sheriff... The 'former' Sheriff and a drug gang were in league with each other. I had for some time suspected that something was wrong, but it proved difficult to find any evidence. Sadly, your brother did come across some information which he passed on to the police...well to me actually.'

Taylor paused for a moment before continuing, 'This was communicated, unbeknown to me, onto the drug gang and Danny and his family were killed in retribution and to silence him. I think that Lawson was the one who gave up his name. I'm truly sorry Adam.'

Adam carelessly dropped the shirts which he had begun folding onto the top of his bag. A deep chill coursed through his body. He turned back to the Sheriff and said sadly, 'I suspected as much.'

'You will be happy to know that the killers and their accomplices are all dead now.' Raising his eyebrows momentarily he continued, 'My report details an attack on their camp at the old Barker place. They were all killed. No evidence has been found to show who the killers were, but it was probably a rival drug gang or members of a south American drug cartel who they dealt with. The Sheriff who was also involved in the drug running was found at his home. It looks like whoever conducted the killings made a particular example of him. We did receive an anonymous tip off in the post informing us of the Barker place and its actual use just prior to these events. I suspected that it came from Lawson who seemed to want 'everyone' killed if they had any connection to the death of Wade, however tenuous that connection was.'

'Thank you for informing me, Sheriff.' Adam replied as he smiled inwardly at the official story that Jervis had constructed to bury the matter.

The Marine then questioned, 'Were you out hunting yesterday, Sheriff?'

The Sheriff gave him a steely look and said, 'Yes. But there was no game to be found, so I just killed some vermin.'

After a pause the Sheriff said, 'Paul is being buried tomorrow. I hope that you can come.'

'Yes, I will be there. He was a great guy!'

The Sheriff frowned and then smiled at Adam and said, 'See you then!'

The officer turned to go and then said, 'Oh and just in case I don't get the chance to speak to you again before you leave ...Good luck in the future and thanks for all you have done!'

Jervis did not elaborate about what the thanks were for, but Adam knew anyway. Taylor then gave him a warm smile and headed for his car.

Chapter Twenty-seven
Kerri's House, Clintburg, Kentucky, USA

Two days later Adam took a taxi to the cemetery and walked slowly through the graveyard feeling a chill breeze gusting across his face before it moved on to tickle the branches of the surrounding trees. Each step felt as if his boots were made of lead, only becoming heavier as he neared his family's graveside. His last steps slowed, and his eyes filled with tears as his mind slowly clouded over with happier memories of times gone by. Tears fell from his bowed head and disappeared into the dark, red soil. He remained with his thoughts and what prayers he could muster. Though his family were gone, he had done his duty. It gave him some solace, but it would never be enough.

A burst of bright red shot across the graves. As he followed the streak of colour, he noted that it was a Northern Cardinal in flight. It alighted on a nearby gravestone. The beautifully coloured bird with tufted feathers on its head then let out an enchanting short burst of whistling song. It was a happy sound which he knew so very well. He watched the little creature allowing it to break his train of thought unknowingly and momentarily, before watching it burst off towards a distant tree. He felt the breeze again chilling the tear streaks on his face. Looking down once more at the gravesite, he came to attention and saluted before turning and walking away.

He then made his way to Paul's fresh grave. As he did so he was aware of an increasing chatter among the birdlife as they headed for more sheltered roosts among the trees. Standing to attention he said, 'It was great knowing you buddy!' Then he saluted once more. Doing a pristine about face he walked away, feeling as if a weight had imperceptibly been lightened on his shoulders as he was able to draw some form of closure.

As Adam passed through the open cemetery gates. He noticed the taxi driver leaning against his vehicle taking a long drag on the stub of a cigarette. Seeing Adam, he threw it to the floor and crushed it underfoot. Adam instructed the man to take him to Kerri's house and they both climbed back into the vehicle. He was nearly overcome by the stench of stale smoke which permeated the car. Adam ran the window down and as the cemetery disappeared from his view cool, fresh air filed the car and allowing him to breathe again.

Kerri knew he would be coming, and she was waiting on the porch with her daughter when he arrived. The shock of what had happened had, to some extent, subsided and a deep sense of relief had overwhelmed her and her daughter. Though she looked happy to see Adam he could tell that she was sad behind the facade. He asked the driver to wait and grabbing his rucksack he went over to see them both to say his goodbyes. Kerri had not wondered why he carried the small rucksack, rather than leaving it in the vehicle. Adam said, 'You guys are looking great!'

Kerri replied dejectedly, 'We are fine now but we are still getting over the ordeal.'

'Time will help you forget.' Adam said, considering the impact of that statement on himself.

'Have you ever thought of moving away and starting again?' He asked.

'Oh Adam,' she sighed longingly, '...we desperately want to leave! But where could we go ...how could we? And ... and there's my Mom. We would never leave her.'

'No, I understand!' he replied consolingly, 'But maybe something will turn up one day?'

'Yes ...sure. I'm sure things will look up soon.' She responded with tears in her eyes and a forced smile as her arm slid around Staci pulling her ever closer.

Adam stepped forward and putting a hand on Kerri's arm he squeezed gently as he kissed her on the cheek.

'I'm sorry but I've got to go now. I am sure things are going to work out for the best.'

He dropped to one knee and gave Staci a peck on the cheek and said, 'Look after your Mum and make sure she keeps out of the sun. She's fair skinned!'

They both looked askance as Adam stood up and asked, 'Can I use the restroom before I go?'

'Sure!' Kerri said as he walked past her.

Adam disappeared into the house briefly and when he returned, he kissed Staci on the cheek again and wished her well. Then, he turned to Kerri and gave her a big hug and kissed her briefly on the lips. Kerri looked surprised as he turned and ran down the steps laughingly calling over his shoulder, 'I hope you enjoy those Keys!'

The bemused Kerri did not have time to ask him what he meant as his door shut, and the driver sped off. Tears ran down her face as she saw the taxi disappearing off onto the highway amid clouds of dust kicked up by the tyres. Kerri breathed in deeply taking in the scent of Adam's aftershave that hung in the air. She thought dejectedly to herself, 'Life just can't get much worse!'

Going back into her home with her daughter she saw the rucksack on the table. Kerri had not noticed that after he had used the restroom, he did not have the rucksack with him when he left. She chided herself for not catching him before he departed. Walking towards the table she could see that beside the bag lay an envelope with 'Kerri' scrawled across the front in blue ink. Opening it she read the letter. Adam had written that he cared for her and her daughter very deeply, but he went no further than that. Then he went on to explain that there was a present in the bag and that it would help make things better. Adam wrote that he also felt that the warm sun would help with her mother's medical conditions. She slowly opened the backpack and found masses of blocks of used dollar bills in many denominations and the details of a quaint, little house in the Florida Keys. Written across the particulars was a note stating that the house had been reserved for her and was ready to be transferred into her name at any point, at no cost.

Kerri turned back to the window and looking out of it at the empty road before she smiled the happiest of happy smiles. Dropping to her knees she cuddled her daughter warmly as she broke down in tears of joy. Kissing her and running her hand through Staci's hair she said, 'A handsome prince has just changed our lives forever! We are going to go on a magical journey with grandma and we will have the happy ever after I thought would never come.'

Chapter Twenty-eight
Wheeler-Sack Army Airfield, Fort Drum, New York State, USA

Adam settled into his seat on the greyhound bus and gradually drifted off. Though he would hardly have called his sleeping arrangements truly comfortable he enjoyed the deepest sleep that he had had in weeks. The journey took many hours with transfers, but Adam felt at ease, even though the pain of his loss would never go. At the penultimate bus station, he called through to Fort Drum and arranged a lift from the terminal back to the camp.

Adam was surprised to find that once more it was Chantel who was driving the Humvee which pulled up at the sidewalk. He found her even more chatty and happier than before. He also sensed that driver felt that she was a party to a rather intimate secret. Warm, comforting air gusted through the open windows as they travelled.

Once more he was to be billeted for the night in the same barracks with the 10th Mountain Division. As Chantel pulled up at the barracks Sara emerged from the building bearing the prettiest of smiles which made her eyes sparkle like brilliant diamonds. As she walked towards him Adam noticed a more feminine sway in her gait.

'Please follow me Sergeant,' she grinned. He grabbed his bag, thanked Chantel, who giggled, and then turned and followed Sara.

She led him to his room, opened the door and unusually strode in ahead of him. He followed her in and softly pushed the door shut dropping his kit bag as he did so. She turned towards him and though her glowing face looked nervous she boldly stepped directly in front of him.

As his arms gently came up to embrace her, Sara's own arms shot forward and pulled him towards her. He was tall and she could feel that he was powerful. She slowly ran her hands across his muscled back feeling at ease. She looked longingly into his eyes as she pulled her body almost onto tiptoes pushing forward to kiss him full on the lips.

Drifting away into his own thoughts as she kissed him back, Adam detected the faintest exotic scent of bergamot and jasmine which made her even more alluring. Just before he had arrived, she had sprayed the scent around her ears and on her wrists. It was her favourite perfume - Dior's J'Adore, Eau de Parfum. She hadn't wished to leave anything to chance.

They kissed for several minutes before gently pulling apart and whilst still embracing looked into each other's eyes. 'Hello Sara!' He whispered.

She softly replied, 'Hello Adam.' Just before she broke into a wide grin.

Sara Tanaka had broken up with her long-term boyfriend more than a year before. She questioned if she would ever get over him. She looked at Adam, completely entranced and she wondered no more.

Sara had already prearranged leave in the hope that things would work out between them. Adam and Sara headed out the next day on a week-long trip through Vermont, New Hampshire, and Maine.

They were both happier than they had been in a long time and their troubles, though not gone, were temporarily forgotten whilst in each other's company.

The two of them greatly enjoyed their time together and had so many happy memories. But among them, they had the most magical evening eating clams and lobster on the terrace of Spinney's restaurant at Popham Beach watching the sunset slip away. They chatted and laughed for what seemed like hours as they drank their way easily through a chilled bottle of Californian Zinfandel.

They returned to Fort Drum happier than when they

had left. Both, in their own way, felt tinged with sadness as they knew they must part.

Chief arrived the next day and he was billeted with Adam for the night. He went for a drink with Adam at a local bar. The marines spent the evening reminiscing, laughing, and enjoying the feel and taste of the ice-cold Coors. The happy evening further helped Adam to forget some of his pain and to prepare for his return to his comrades.

The next morning Sara drove Adam to the waiting Lockheed C-5M Super Galaxy whilst Chantel drove Chief to the bus station. Adam and Sara had already said their goodbyes in private and their final parting was quite formal as he turned and climbed the ramp of the waiting transporter. Adam looked back at Sara longingly, and he thought to himself that she looked slightly teary eyed as he waved and gave her a final smile before doing an about face and disappearing into the vast aircraft.

He looked from the window and saw Sara some distance away watching the aircraft. She did not waive, though she watched until the Lockheed had taxied out to the main runway heading on its way to RAF Brize Norton in the UK. She walked back to the vehicle looking up as she did, so that tears would not fall. Climbing back into her vehicle and deeply saddened, Sara turned on some music. The song, 'Sukiyaki' or as she preferred to call it 'Ue o Muite Arukō', sang out. The sweetly lyrical voice of the long dead singer, Kyu Sakamoto, touched her soul as tears welled up uncontrollably in her pretty eyes before bursting forth and tracing their cruel path across her soft cheeks. As Sara looked through the windscreen watching Adam's plane climb beyond the clouds, her heart broken, she whispered, 'Sayonara, my love!'

Exhausted, Adam slipped into a deep sleep in the aircraft.

The flight was uneventful and after a brief stop in England he was flown on to Afghanistan. Back to the comfort and familiarity of his rifle and of his scope – back to the next kill – the next 'Eye Kill'!

Adam was decorated twice more before he finished his tour in Afghanistan. He eventually shipped out, back to the States. Shortly afterwards he left the US military.

Chapter Twenty-nine
Whitehead Street, Old Town, Key West, Florida, USA

Kerri walked beside her mother, helping her across the hardwood floor heading out through the solid Mahogany front door with its three elegant, bevelled glass panels along the top. They deftly made their way down the steps and through the small front garden before exiting via the open gate. The house was fronted by a low stone wall surmounted by a white picket fence. Kerri called back to her daughter, 'Hurry up, Staci!'

Moments later the young girl's footsteps could be heard running through and then out of the house before slowing into a gentle, contented skip, eventually coming to a stop at the side of the two women.

'Great we're ready then!' The photographer, who stood before them, chuckled.

He nonchalantly stepped back into the quiet road as he fiddled with his camera.

Turning to the trio he suggested, 'I think it would be sensible if I have Mom in the middle and you two young girls either side.'

They smiled to each other on hearing, Dave, the photographer's complimentary words.

Kerri moved to the other side of Madison, her Mom, and they all cuddled up close, with the quaint, little house in the background. It was constructed of wood and close boarded with three large windows. To the front it had a narrow porch with white painted wooden uprights supporting the shingle roof. Much of the detailing on the house was picked out in white, though the boarding was painted in a rich, pastel lemon. Dotted inside the picket fence in the compact garden were several small palm trees which gently swayed in the light breeze. The welcome gusts gave some respite in the heat of the day. The lush green fronds chattered away, as they flapped against each other under a clear blue sky. The sound of the windchime in motion, and the smell of the sea lent a certain magic to the moment. Kerri and Staci had made the windchime from seashells picked up on the shoreline and it proudly hung below the porch roof for all to see.

The photographer readied his camera and kindly ordered, 'Come on girls! Show me those beautiful smiles!'

The air was alive with the smell of exotic flowers which peppered the surrounding gardens. The warmth, the breeze caressing their skin, the beauty, the colours, and the location added a sprinkle of magical fairy dust to the whole occasion - one that they would remember forever.

They stopped their chatter and turned towards the camera bursting with contentment and joy.

The cameraman grabbed his chance and snapped away, capturing a moment in time for the happy family which they could never have dreamed would actually come.

As Dave packed his equipment away he said, 'I'll get the photos to you next week.' Then, smiling he continued, 'I'll drop them by myself.'

Kerri's face lit up as she replied, 'Yes, you do that!'

Chapter Thirty
La Jolla, San Diego, California, USA

In a quieter, slightly less affluent side street of the fashionable La Jolla district of San Diego a dark Buick pulled up at the curb side. A tall solidly built man with dark skin stepped out of the car. Before closing the door, he grabbed a brown parcel from inside. His eyes were shielded by dark sunglasses as he looked around scanning the street. He was dressed much the same as many Americans dress, in sneakers, blue-jeans and a faded yellow T-shirt. However, he also had an ankle holster with a small handgun secreted inside it and covered by the denim. He saw what he was looking for and then walked along the street and up two steps before ringing the doorbell. As he waited, he glanced around cautiously - a habit he could not shift.

A moment later the door was opened by Perveen. Seeing the man who appeared to be Middle Eastern she looked terrified and took a sharp intake of breath. Her eight-year-old son Faraj who was nearby saw that his mother was distressed. He bravely ran in front of her and held Perveen against him to try to protect her. He looked at the man with a strong steely face, but still the face of a child. But then there was recognition, as Faraj stared at him before breaking into a wide smile and shouting out, 'Chief!'

He ran to the Marine with open arms. Chief had dropped to his knee and clasped the young boy to him saying, 'It's great to see you again Faraj!'

Then Chief looked up at the boy's mother who, though she was still nervous, had a soft smile on her face – a smile of relief. Chief continued to hold the boy, then he picked the parcel up which he had just dropped and passed it to Perveen. Then continuing with a smile, he happily said, 'This is a gift from a friend of your husband's, Adam. Welcome to America!'

He gently pushed Faraj away still holding the boy's shoulders and looked into his eyes saying solemnly, 'All of us in the unit really liked your father,' he then looked up at Perveen saying, '...your husband. His loss was a heavy blow to us all.'

The tender gesture by the burly marine had a profound effect on little Faraj, who had felt as if his life had disintegrated beyond repair with the loss of his beloved father.

Returning his gaze to Faraj the Marine continued, 'Amit was a very brave man.' As Chief said the words the boy's eyes grew watery and his gaze dropped towards the floor. His mother stretched out her hand and rubbed Faraj's back tenderly before Chief went on, 'We owe your father an enormous debt of gratitude and we will repay it to you all.'

He gently pulled Faraj to him and hugged him tenderly.

'Hey wait a minute!' He continued, 'I had a few more things in my car, that I need to get.'

Chief jumped up and slipped down the stairs and back to the car. He grabbed two small bicycles, a basketball hoop and a basketball from the trunk and walked back smiling. As he came closer to the door, he called out, 'What self-respecting young child would be without a basketball court. As he reached the door, he said to the boy who stood staring with wide eyes, 'I can fit this up now if you want?'

Looking up to his mother, Faraj said, 'Yes please.'

She stepped back into the hall and welcomed Chief in, and then the little boy showed him through to the garden at the back of the house. Chief went over to the shed at the bottom of the garden and pulled out a short ladder and some tools and then quickly fitted the hoop to the house wall, while the little boy's sisters excitedly pushed themselves around on their new balance bikes.

Chief finished his work and replaced the ladder and tools after which he began to shoot hoops with Faraj.

Occasionally, in happier times, Faraj would come to the base in Afghanistan with his father, Amit. He would play baseball and basketball with the troops and would sometimes practice catch with an American football. Chief remembered that one of the soldiers had given Faraj a San Francisco 49ers shirt which he wore whenever he came. He would leave the shirt at the army camp, as to bring it home may have caused him difficulties in his community. Both Perveen and Chief looked with great joy at the happy little boy as he ran about the yard and took shots.

Forty minutes later the boy's mother came into the garden with a pot of 'Kahwah' and two glasses which she placed on a simple wooden table which lay to the side near the fence. It was delicious and made of green tea, cardamom, cinnamon and saffron. The exotic smell of it instantly took the marine back to the bazaars of Kabul. Moments later she returned with a large plate of 'Sheer Payra' – a traditional rosewater and cardamom fudge from Afghanistan. On seeing this the three children stopped playing and raced over to the plate to take handfuls of the fudge which they quickly consumed. Perveen sat down and poured the tea and offered the sheer payra to Chief. He knew the delicacy well and gratefully took two pieces. As he ate them Perveen said, 'Thank you for your kindness and the kindness of the other marines. It has been very difficult recently.'

He noted that her English was good and almost at the level which her husband had achieved. She was well educated, which was not an easy thing for a woman to have achieved given the political climate in her country.

Taking a sip of the tea Chief replied compassionately, 'We were all struck by the loss of Amit and by his selfless bravery. Please do not worry about the future for you and your children. All of us will do our best to help you. Remember our motto in the marines is 'Semper Fidelis' – Always Faithful!'

Her beautiful almond shaped eyes were moist with tears though she smiled softly in thanks.

As he looked at her, he couldn't help but be struck by her charm and her beauty. She was an attentive and kindly host despite the horrors and the upheaval that she had faced. He also noticed that whenever she came close to him, he was sure that he could smell the faintest hint of frankincense.

The two of them sat relaxing at the table as they watched the children who had started playing again. He truly enjoyed the taste of the sweet fudge that she had served with its unusual, middle eastern flavours. Then she turned towards Chief as he pulled a sheet of paper from his pocket which he handed to her, 'This is Adam's cell number and mine as well. If you have any difficulties, then please contact us. But don't worry we will be checking in on you all every now and again.'

The basketball came bouncing towards the table followed closely by Faraj. Chief's face grew stern as he looked at the boy, though he continued with a happy voice and a wagging finger, 'Now make sure that you look after your mom and your sisters and work hard at school!'

Faraj cheerily nodded his head in response.

'I need to go now, but it's wonderful seeing you again.' He said kindly.

Then turning to the boy's mother, he thanked her for her hospitality and gave her a small envelope. Perveen showed him to the door and as he left, he gave them a wave goodbye. The boy was sad to see him go and as Chief jumped into his car and drove away Faraj watched and waved vigorously. As the vehicle disappeared around the corner Perveen opened the envelope and found a photograph of Amit surrounded by his Marine friends in happier times.

Shutting the door, they returned to the kitchen and opened the present from Adam. Perveen and Faraj stood there unmoving, stunned to see such a large pile of varying denominations of used dollar bills bursting from the box before them.

Two days later an Amazon truck pulled up outside their new home and Faraj received a box with his name on it. Inside he found an American football and a San Francisco 49ers shirt.

As Faraj tried his shirt on his mother looked at the gift note which came with the present. It said simply, 'Semper Fi!'

Perveen was unable to hold the tears back, as she gently ran her finger across the words caressing them as she did so. But the warm tears that slid down her face and which fell to the floor, exploding as they landed, were tears of hope and happiness.

Chapter Thirty-one
The Courthouse, Clintburg, Kentucky, USA

A warm breeze blew across the square which fronted the courthouse. The building had stood sentinel in the centre of Clintburg for over a century. Nobody sat on the public benches, and nobody walked the streets. It was far too hot! The few people to be seen about, were driving their cars, sat in diners, or they were leisurely strolling around shops – all were cool, and all of them were thoroughly air-conditioned.

Built in the Greek Revival style with a prominent cupola, the vast, white, legal structure was a source of great civic pride for the people of the small Kentucky town.

Within its walls only three of the six available courtrooms were in session. Court 1, Judge Browning's court, as it was still known, lay idle as he had retired some months before. By all accounts he had disappeared off to an island far to the south in more tropical climes. He had been well liked by the staff and the other Judges and though they were happy for him, they couldn't help but feel a little envious.

Judge Dickerson sat in Court 2, embroiled in a particularly messy case about the alleged theft of a river boat. He would eventually adjourn the matter, to arrange a site visit to better acquaint himself with the facts. His interest piqued in all things boating, he would later find himself reading Jerome K. Jerome's Three Men in a Boat during his lunchbreaks.

Court 3 was presided over by the highly respected Judge Weston. She was the longest serving female Judge in the state. Along with Clintburg's second female who sat in Court 4, Judge Sturmenkovic, they made a formidable team.

The final Court in use, number 5, was the preserve of Judge Atkinson. In the last week that he sat before he too retired, the Judge presided over a mixed bag of cases which were not overly taxing for a man of his stature. The listing officer had wanted to give the kindly Judge a relaxing week to remember.

Court 6 hadn't been used in years, except once as a film set which had created great excitement at the courthouse.

Judge Atkinson's penultimate case involved a young man who had been indicted on various charges. They related to the accused's low-level role on the periphery of a large-scale drug gang which had operated in the state, and which had involved criminals and corrupt police officers. It had been sensationalised in the media, both locally and nationally, following the brutal slaughter of most of those involved. The killers had not been apprehended though it was widely believed that contract killers in the employ of a Mexican or a Columbian cartel were responsible.

Everyone in the community expressed horror and outrage outwardly. However, there was widespread relief, verging on elation, in some quarters that the individuals and their criminal operation were gone.

Having helpfully left multiple, incriminatory messages on the deceased Sheriff Carter's phone the former receptionist had little option but to enter a plea of guilty.

Jaxon's lawyer had mitigated on his behalf, as best he could. Though the defendant's previous good character was very thin on the ground.

The defendant was in shock, and he was terrified of going to prison even though it had been inevitable. The Judge considered the facts and what little mitigation there was, he also considered the man who stood before him and the crimes he had committed. Then he handed down his judgement – as always considered, fair and just.

Judge Atkinson had recommended him as suitable for a minimum-security institution, the Blackburn Correctional Complex in Lexington. The Judge had seen something unsaid, in Jaxon – a true sense of regret and contrition and Atkinson had felt that with help the defendant might well change. The sentence was to prove life changing for the former pot smoking motel clerk.

The prison's 'Thoroughbred Retirement Foundation' program provided care for retired racing horses. The prison farm program had been a huge success with the rehabilitation of prisoners. Nestled amid the bluegrass of Kentucky and based in a converted old dairy barn the former receptionist had truly connected with the creatures.

In particular, he had formed a great affection for a handsome old grey called Monty. This, coupled with his enrolment in the Alcoholics and Narcotics Anonymous programme, which was run by the prison, profoundly altered the course of his life in a positive way. The young man went on to take courses in watercolours and graphic design which he found therapeutic.

Jaxon's world had opened up, in a way that would have been impossible if he had remained amidst his former colleagues. One day, nearing the end of his sentence Jaxon took Monty for a walk from the stables to a small paddock where he could meander through the bluegrass to his hearts content. He had done so many times before. Entering the small field, he released the lead rope from the head collar and watched happily as Monty turned and nuzzled him gently before trotting off. Jaxon thought to himself, 'Soon I will be released too Monty!'

The sky was full of great cumulous clouds which gently drifted across a deep blue sky, casting vast shadows over the landscape as they passed by. Jaxon breathed in deeply as the light breeze pushed past him, leaving him invigorated. One of the warders had contacted some friends of his who said that they would hire the young man once he was released. The former receptionist felt that life, which had always dealt him a bad hand, had begun to feed him Aces. He was determined to never fail again.

Jaxon smiled to himself as he wandered after Monty and began to think of the new life which lay ahead of him. A better life.

On the former Judges first day of retirement, he had woken early and made macchiato coffees for himself and his wife. The pervasive smell of the exotic Jamaica Blue Mountain coffee was intoxicating. Then he had settled into his favourite comfy chair in preparation to proofread his friend's new manuscript. The story needed work, and the novelist needed support and encouragement and the kindly Judge, and his wife were happy to help. He glanced at the title page of the thriller, before flicking it over and beginning to read the prologue.

Before he had finished the first paragraph, his wife, who was savouring her coffee while looking at her own copy, questioned, 'Did you know that he is working on a new book called, 'Eight jackboots for Masca? He said that it will be his first foray into the horror genre. What on earth do you think the title alludes to?'

The Judge laughed, rolled his eyes, and cryptically replied, 'I dread to think! But when we proofread it, then I suspect we may have to make the macchiato's ... doubles!'

Smiling and feeling the comforting warmth of the coffee cup in his hand he turned back to the manuscript and started to read once more.

Judge Atkinson was never to know of the role that his judgement had taken in the positive process which transformed Jaxon's life. He, like the other Judges, had purely performed his duties with professionalism, intelligence, and compassion for both the victims and the defendants.

Chapter Thirty-two
Légion étrangère, Caserne Joffre, Rue Jean
Vieilledent, Perpignan, France

Adam arrived the night before. He had taken the train
from Paris and had stepped out on a balmy evening onto
the platform of the Gare de Perpignan. He could have
signed on in Paris, but he had chosen to go to Perpignan
because one of his friends from the Marines had, some
years before, signed on there. He walked from the train
station through the historic centre for just over a mile
until he came to the hotel he had previously booked, Le
Mas des Arcades.

Adam was tired. He had been travelling for two days
and had not slept much. So, after booking in he went
straight to bed. He woke early, feeling the heat of the sun
on his face as warm beams burst through a crack in the
curtains.

Adam showered quickly and then slipped down the

stairs in swimming trunks and a bathrobe and went for a morning swim in the pool which lay next to the hotel. The water was very refreshing and relaxing after the stifling heat of the night. He swam half a mile front crawl and then relaxed in the water for ten minutes. He was the only person in the pool as the other residents had not risen. Adam returned to his room, dressed, and packed the little luggage which he had before heading to breakfast. The staff were helpful and friendly and seemed pleased when he tried to speak the little French which he knew. Adam took his time with breakfast as he was in no great hurry. He finished his coffee as other sleepy residents began to make their way into the room. They were very polite, and all wished him, he believed as it was said in French, good morning. Finishing, he grabbed his bag and went to the front desk.

The receptionist was very French and very attractive, and he found her most attentive. At his request she gave him directions to an internet cafe and from there to the Legion recruiting office. As he left, she gave him the warmest of smiles and wished him, 'Bonne chance!'

He took a leisurely stroll into town and shortly after turning into the quaint Place Hyacinthe Rigaud he wandered into the 'Café Afrique', a cyber cafe. Adam paid for half an hour on one of the computers to give him access to his emails. There was nothing of importance though an email from Kerri caught his eye. It was a long email with pictures attached. As he read through it a gentle smile crossed his face. Kerri spoke of her new life in Florida. Her mother's health was improving, and her daughter was enjoying the new school where she had made many friends. She explained that they had settled in well in Key West in a quiet suburb not far from the beach. She spoke of her gratitude to Adam and her deep affection for him. The attached pictures were of a happy little family on the beach standing proudly in front of their new home. Adam thought to himself that this was a perfect way to start his day and his new life in France. He wrote a short email back to Kerri and wished her and her family well. He explained that he was in France though he did not say why. Adam finished up and then left the internet cafe and walked to the Rue Jean Vielledent.

He stopped momentarily at the corner of the street to collect his thought, before entering the Caserne Joffre to sign up at the Foreign Legion recruiting office for the obligatory five years.

As Adam waited, he saw a slightly built, dark skinned, young man holding a map and looking about as if he was lost. He noticed Adam and walked over to him carrying a broad smile as he did so. Adam thought that he had a kindly face as he enquired very politely, 'Please sir, can you help me? I want to join the Foreign Legion. Where is it please?'

He spoke in heavily accented, though clear, English. Adam wondered if the young man really knew what he was letting himself in for, but he replied, 'Come with me! I'm going there myself. My name is Adam. I'm American,'

Adam stretched out his arm and they shook hands as the young man, who looked very relieved, said, 'Thank you! My name is Sarath. I am from India.'

They walked on through the great pillars that marked the entrance to the Foreign Legion base. The tough looking guards eyed them warily but, without speaking, pointed them onwards to a nondescript doorway which led into a large building nearby.

They entered and immediately came upon a gruff looking Brigadier-chef, a senior corporal, who was sat at a desk in the middle of the room. He eyed them both with disdain and said something rapidly in French which Adam did not catch. So, he replied in English, 'We are here to join the Foreign Legion.'

The corporal looked them up and down, paying particular attention to the wiry Sarath before saying in rough English, 'We'll see about that!'

He continued, 'Are you together?'

Sarath looked nervous and was about to say something when Adam butted in, 'Yes we are!'

Sarath looked back at him and smiled warmly.

Adam did not know it then, but his newfound acquaintance would end up being one of his closest friends and the very reason that he would visit a place he thought he would never go – the mysterious, Western Ghats.

Epilogue
Years later, Beirut, Lebanon, Middle East

Beirut, once known as 'The Paris of the Middle East', was, sadly, but a shadow of its former self.

In a non-descript building, in a shabby street, in an ugly district of that once great city a young man stood before a rough-hewn wooden table. He had travelled for many weeks to get there from his home in the distant mountains of Afghanistan. The journey had been gruelling and fraught with danger. He read the document that lay in front of him before, smiling as he did so, signing its last page. Handing it back to the old man who sat before him, the boy who had become a man turned and left the Beirut office of the Red Crescent humanitarian organisation – it's newest recruit.

Stepping out into the hot, dusty, tree-lined thoroughfare he took in a long, slow, deep breath. He felt at ease with himself, as if a long-cherished dream had eventually come to fruition. The curious smell of spices and pollution was overpowering. He took in his surroundings and then looked up at the clear blue sky through the gently fluttering leaves. As he did so, Omar remembered years before, as a child, looking up into the hills of his homeland and into a sniper's rifle and watching as that Marine took his finger away from the trigger.

Ever since, he had dedicated himself to peace and humanity and that day in a dusty Beirut suburb was the culmination of his quest.

AFTERWORD

Thank you for taking the time to read or listen my book. I hope that you enjoyed it.

You can greatly help me and potential new readers by leaving a review. As long or as short a review as you wish would be great.

I read all reviews and greatly appreciate the time and effort that my readers go to in leaving them.

If you wish to join my mailing list to be among the first to hear about forthcoming books and deals, then please sign up at: **www.idograf.com**

Thank you

Ido Graf

About the Author

Ido Graf grew up in the Mediterranean and in the United Kingdom, predominantly in London.

After studying for a bachelor's degree, Ido went on to study for a masters, before taking other specialist qualifications.

He spent considerable time in military bases in Europe and the Middle East and comes from a police & military background.

Ido has travelled extensively in North & South America, Europe, Africa, the Far East, Russia, and the former Eastern bloc countries.

He was questioned at length in Guinea by the Presidential Guard on spying allegations relating to the Presidential

Palace and in Sierra Leone by agents of the state concerning alleged diamond smuggling.

Ido and a friend of his once engaged in a shooting competition in the Củ Chi district of Ho Chi Minh City, with John F. Kennedy while Jr. Daryl Hannah watched the three of them as they fired AK-47s. It was an extraordinary, chance encounter when they were travelling in Vietnam in the 1990s.

Ido is a fully qualified scuba diver and skydiver. He is a proficient snowboarder, skier (both downhill and cross-country) and a highly experienced alpinist.

He has worked in various sectors for both government departments and private concerns in a variety of sensitive fields in the UK and North America.

Ido Graf is a writer of mystery and suspense thrillers. His works, which he is now publishing, are derived from his own experiences and from meticulous research. He visits all the locations that he writes about to maintain the highest standards of realism within his novels.

Though much of his output is contemporary in nature, it frequently has a historical basis at its core.

The focus of his books is in the political, corporate espionage, thriller, and adventure categories.

He hopes that you enjoy his novels. Please follow Ido Graf on his blog:

https://www.idograf.com

Acknowledgements

It is no easy task to write a novel. Each of these people or groups have had an impact on my writing and on my will to write.

On some occasions, they may have felt that their contribution was minimal, but their impact was tremendous and at some moments, crucial.

Special thanks for their support, critical appraisal, guidance and encouragement:

Family and friends including

My darling wife and my sons

Andy & Gerlinde, Mark, David & Kerri, Ian, K.W.,

S.A.S.

John & Tammy

Paul & Gwyneth

Inspirations

The many authors of fiction which I have read including, among others, such greats as Graham Greene, John le Carré, Frederick Forsyth, Nelson DeMille, Robert Harris, John Grisham, Jack Higgins, Mark Dawson, Thomas Hardy, Evelyn Waugh, Desmond Bagley, Hammond Innes, Helen MacInnes, Alistair MacLean, Robert Wilson, Randy Wayne White and most of all the works and inspiring life journey of Lee Child.

The kindness, encouragement and tutoring of novelists: Frederick E. Smith and Rosemary Aitken.

Also

Special thanks go to those people, some I may never even have known or met, throughout my life who have extended to me - kindness, support and assistance even though, on occasion, there was no reason to have expected it.

Any successes in my writing are built on the shoulders of those mentioned above, any faults solely my own.